Menopause, Moon Magic, & Cursed Kisses

Menopause, Magick, & Mystery, Volume 4

JC BLAKE

Published by Redbegga Publishing, 2021.

This is a work of fiction. Similarities to real people, places, or events are entirely coincidental.

MENOPAUSE, MOON MAGIC, & CURSED KISSES

First edition. March 29, 2021.

Copyright © 2021 JC BLAKE.

Written by JC BLAKE.

To all women, may you forever hold magick in your hearts.

Chapter One

On the morning that the invitation for the wedding was hand-delivered, the atmosphere at Haligern Cottage was tense. Aunt Loveday had been unable to repair a crack in the stone mantle above the hearth in the kitchen and Uncle Raif's health had taken a turn for the worse. Rolling fog hovered across the lawn and blotted the early autumn sunlight. The kitchen was dingey with shadows hugging the corners. With the fire unlit, I shivered, zipped my fleece, filled the kettle, then busied myself with lighting the fire. Despite the crack in the stone slab the fire was still in use, although finding it unlit at this time, particularly on a such a cold morning, was unusual. The other peculiarity in the room was the lack of aunts.

Minutes passed and I sipped freshly made coffee alone. Ticking from the grandfather clock in the hallway punctuated the silence with each tick growing more distinct as I looked out across the garden through the kitchen window. Even the familiars were missing.

Mornings would generally be a mess of bustling activity with my aunts gathered in the kitchen chattering about which herbs to collect next according to which phase the moon was in and which charm would suit it best. Should they try one of Euphemia's for the mugwort this time? Or one from Thomasin's grimoire for the plantain? Bess, Aunt Beatrice's highly strung whippet familiar would trot into the kitchen then yelp as Benny, Aunt Thomasin's midnight-black raven, swooped from a high shelf to peck at her rump. Inevitably she would bump into Lucifer who would hiss, take a swipe at her with his paw, then spring after her. Benny would return to a higher shelf or hop to the back of a chair, beady black eyes watching the fun, waiting for another opportunity to peck a rump. Sometimes he would even fly down to sit on their backs, talons gripping their fur, until he was flung off like a cowboy at a rodeo. Chaos would generally ensue with Bess and Lucifer running between our ankles and darting under the table until one of us opened the door and shooed the trio of cavorting creatures out into the garden.

Several days ago, Renweard, a lolloping Wolfhound puppy, had been added to the bubbling pot of familiar energy. Thankfully, he was often asleep beside the hearth or sat quietly at Aunt Loveday's side. Benny, happy to share his talents, was not averse to pecking Renweard on the rump too, and then the kitchen would erupt as the oversized and lolloping puppy skidded around the floor chasing Bess, Lucifer, and Benny until Aunt Loveday cast a calming spell and I opened the door to the garden.

This morning the kitchen was chaos-free and, as I sipped my coffee in silence, I missed the chatter, the clatter of pans, the tacking of claws across the floor, and the excited yelps and hisses of the familiars at play. At that moment I would even have welcomed a fairy, the sense of disquiet was so oppressive.

I sighed, placed my cup on its saucer and gazed across the garden. Apart from the fog it too was empty, and I was about to return upstairs and search for my aunts when Lucifer strolled into the kitchen.

"Lucifer!" I said in an overly effusive tone.

"Liv!" His reply was dour and disinterested. He padded across to the hearth, sniffed at the cold air, swished his tail, and stropped over to his bowl.

"Do you want some breakfast?"

Lucifer stared at the empty bowl.

"Not hungry."

This was a first! "Not hungry? Are you sure? I have some salmon. You can have some if you like?"

He swished his tail in annoyance.

"Port? Would you like some port?"

For a moment he glanced at me but then only sniffed at the air. "Not today."

Lucifer never missed an opportunity to have a saucer of port and particularly revelled in coercing me into giving him some in the mornings. Generally, I held off, and we would have a drink together in the evening, he with a saucer of port, I with a glass of red, preferably a Chianti or Rioja Reserva. Refusing the drink was unheard of. "Lucifer ... what's wrong?"

"I'm just not in the mood."

Since the crack in the mantle had appeared, and we had realised the coven was under attack, the energy in the house had changed, but it wasn't until Uncle Raif had become unwell that a sense of oppression tinged with despair had descended over our home.

"Hmm, I know what you mean."

Lucifer sat beside the bowl, tail curled around his feet, then stared off into the distance. "I think I shall take a walk," he stated then plodded with a defeated air to the door.

"Great idea," I said with enthusiasm I didn't feel.

Lucifer sidled across the flagstones then disappeared into the fog hovering over the lawn without a single dismissive word or derisive glance in my direction. I sighed, closed the door, and decided that if I didn't do something to lift the mood, we would all slip into a quagmire of misery.

The crunch of gravel alerted me to a visitor and I almost ran to the front door, flinging it open with relief to a man with his fist raised and ready to knock.

"Oh!" he said with a bemused laugh, no doubt shocked by the swinging door and the sudden appearance of a dumpy, dishevelled, wild-eyed, and breathless woman. "Good morning," he offered, recovering quickly. "On behalf of Lady Heskitt, I am delivering an invitation for ..." he looked down at the large cream envelope in his hand, "Mr. Raif Wolfreston." He offered a smile but not the envelope. In smart navy slacks and white shirt beneath a navy cable-knit sweater, he towered above me with assured calm.

I suddenly realised how unkempt my appearance was in comparison to his. A waft of pleasant and manly cologne that reminded me of Pascal rose between us and I regretted not having brushed my hair that morning. In my defence, I hadn't slept well, and dreams of a dark and malignant presence had infused my waking moments. Nevertheless, my aunts always managed to look elegant and collected, even in their most casual moments. I had to up my game!

"Is Mr. Wolfreston in?"

"Oh! Yes. I mean no."

A quizzical frown replaced his smile. "Well, can I leave the invitation with you?"

"I ... yes, of course. Uncle Raif, I mean Mr. Wolfreston is home, he's just not well at the moment," I rambled. This morning my chaotic hormones seemed to have thrown a spanner into the workings of my mind. "So, yes, I can take it to him."

He passed me the envelope and returned to his car, a highly polished and sporty-looking burgundy BMW, and left.

As the car crunched over the gravel and rolled towards the open gate, I examined the envelope. Made of heavyweight manilla paper it was sealed with a dollop of red wax imprinted with the Heskitt seal, an image of the grand Elizabethan frontage of Heskitt Hall circled by their motto. Under ordinary circumstances the invitation would have caused excitement among my aunts, and Uncle Raif, especially, would have been delighted. Charismatic and charming, he was a natural social butterfly and loved company. I held the invitation with a heavy heart—Uncle Raif had to get better!

Closing the door, I turned to slippered footsteps slowly padding down the stairs.

"Uncle Raif!"

Chapter Two

Surprised to see my uncle downstairs, I quickly joined him in the hallway. Apart from his slippers, he was dressed and ready for the day. His white mutton chop whiskers were perfectly groomed, and a slight flush had risen to his cheeks from the exertion of coming down the stairs. It gave a healthier bloom to his skin but couldn't hide the worn and faded look in his eyes. "Why, Livitha!" He took a breath before continuing. "You look beautiful this morning."

I took his hand and leaned in to kiss him. His hand was cool to the touch, the fingers white as though drained of blood. "You look wonderful yourself," I replied.

"Such a big fib, my dear!" His smile was indulgent. "I think a cup of tea is in order." He held his elbow out for me to take. "Shall we?"

"Indeed, we shall," I replied and walked with him through to the kitchen taking slow steps, allowing him to lead.

"Ah!" he sighed with relief as he eased himself down into a chair.

Lucifer appeared close to the hearth and trotted across the floor then jumped onto his lap, curling instantly. Uncle Raif stroked his head with gnarled hands even more aged than yesterday. Trying not to stare, I placed the envelope on the table.

"This came for you this morning," I said with more enthusiasm than I felt. "I think you may like it."

He took the envelope, nodding with approval as he noted the stamped wax seal. "I do like it when they do things properly, none of this licking nonsense. Unhygienic really."

"They make self-sealing envelopes now."

"Quite right, and so they should."

He pulled a pen knife from his pocket and slipped the blade beneath the seal then unfolded the paper. "Well!" he said as he read. "Isn't this marvellous. We have been invited to a wedding!"

"So, are you going to attend?"

"Attend what, Livitha?"

Aunt Loveday stood in the doorway, and breath caught in my chest as I watched her enter the room. She had aged dramatically and had even developed a slight stoop. Walking with slow progress as though each step were painful, she stopped beside Uncle Raif. Renweard, her Wolfhound familiar, took padding steps and sat to attention at her feet.

"Why, we have been invited to the wedding of ... Now, what did it say?" Uncle Raif glanced at the invitation. "Ah, yes. We have been invited to attend the wedding of Lady Annabelle Heskitt and the Right Honourable Tarquin Sotheby-Jones. It would seem that they're cocking a snook at the curse."

That word again! "Curse?" I asked.

"Yes, you know, the Heskitt Curse."

The image of a dark horse bearing a headless rider sprang to mind—the bronze statue at the centre of Heskitt Hall's courtyard. "But that's just a legend, surely. I mean, I always thought it was just a marketing ploy—a curiosity to draw in the tourists.

Lady Heskitt is definitely a savvy businesswoman and she *has* capitalised on the history of Heskitt Hall."

"Capitalised isn't quite how I'd put it," Uncle Raif said in a disapproving voice as Aunt Thomasin entered the room. She was followed by Aunt Euphemia.

"Oh, no, dear. It's definitely real," Aunt Loveday confirmed. "The family were cursed. At least ... I think they were." She stalled with an uncharacteristic frown of confusion then flapped a hand as though batting the struggling memory away. "Well, it was such a long time ago ..."

"Well," said Aunt Thomasin pouring a cup of tea from the pot on the table. "The curse was cast centuries ago now, so I would think it has greatly weakened over time."

"I wouldn't be surprised if it were a dead curse."

"Can curses die? I thought they had to be broken." My query went unheard.

"It could be dead, I suppose," said Aunt Euphemia. "Although it has to be said, that there have been no successful marriages along the female line since that time."

I was unsure what marriage had to do with the Headless Horseman, but the aunts were in full flow so waited for the link to reveal itself in conversation.

"True," said Aunt Thomasin. "There hasn't been a female Heskitt for many generations though, so it's difficult to confirm whether the curse still holds power."

"How long has it been?" asked Uncle Raif. He appeared thoughtful for a moment then said. "Hah! The last girl born to a Heskitt before Lady Annabelle was during Victoria's reign. "Do you remember, dear? We were invited to the Christening. What was her name?"

"Hmm ... Constance. Yes! Constance." Aunt Loveday's eyes sparkled with victory.

"That's right. And she *was* a bonny girl."

"Marriage ended in disaster though."

"Indeed. Terrible business."

"Titanic wasn't it?"

"Yes, they both died."

"And you think that was because of the curse?" I asked, now even more confused. What had the Headless Horseman to do with the Titanic?

"Well, it does fit."

"But the Titanic was an international maritime disaster," I said. "Could a curse do that?"

"Well, some are extremely powerful."

"But so many people died!"

"Sadly, that is true, but curses have no morality, dear," explained Aunt Loveday. "Their only purpose is to harm the recipient. Others that die along the way are just collateral damage."

"I'm not sure the Heskitt curse *is* that strong," added Aunt Thomasin, "but the truth is, if the husband hadn't been trying to flee the country after embezzling rather a lot of money-"

"And stealing her jewels."

"Yes, and stealing her jewels, then neither of them would have been on the ship in the first place."

This explanation left me no closer to understanding the connection between the curse of the Headless Horseman and the Titanic. "So, to be clear, Annabelle Heskitt is the first female to be born to the family since the late-eighteenth century?"

"Yes."

"And you think that she will succumb to the curse?"

"Perhaps."

"Unless it's dead."

"Yes, unless it's dead."

I sighed. I had to clarify the situation. "Aunt Thomasin, what exactly is the curse?"

"Oh! Yes, well it is said to be that no daughter of a firstborn son shall prosper in marriage."

"And Annabelle is the daughter of Sir Lancelot Heskitt who was a firstborn son."

"The temerity!" Grumbled Uncle Raif. "Calling a Heskitt after a true gentleman!"

Aunt Loveday placed a gnarled hand upon his shoulder. He stroked her fingers with his own and grew calm again.

"Now I am confused," I said. "What has that got to do with the horseman?"

"Nothing."

"Nothing?"

"The horseman is a legend that has become confused with the curse."

"But that's what Heskitt Hall is known for. They even have a café named after him. They sell keyrings and mugs in their souvenir shop."

"They do."

"So, there are two different curses?"

"No, only the curse cast over the daughters of first-born sons."

"So, the Headless Horsman of Heskitt Hall is a fake."

"No, he's real."

"At least he was!" piped up Aunt Beatrice. "He was such a good-looking man—such a shame they chopped off his head. It would be rather grand to see him ride again."

"With his head attached, of course," Aunt Euphemia said in earnest.

"Obviously, Euphemia. That goes without saying."

"Didn't you have a crush on him, Beatrice?"

She batted her hand at Aunt Thomasin. "Pah! Well, yes, but that had nothing to do with his terrible and tragic end. I had another lover by the time he was beheaded—so nothing to do with me!"

"A lover?" I asked in surprise.

Aunt Beatrice turned to me with her lips pursed. "Why? Don't you believe I could have had a lover? I was attractive once you know."

"Yes! Yes, of course, but ... it's just-"

Aunt Thomasin chuckled. "Let her be, Beatrice. The poor girl is flustered. Let's get back to Lady Annabelle and her doomed wedding!" Her eyes glittered with mirth.

"Quite right."

"Is her marriage doomed?"

"Probably not."

"I doubt it."

"But it will be interesting to see how it all pans out."

"Indeed, it will. The next decade or so shall tell us the truth."

Decade? I wanted to know now! "Perhaps she doesn't know about the curse," I offered.

"That's possible given the lapse of time since the last female Heskitt married."

"I think that unlikely. She must know."

"But perhaps doesn't believe it?"

"Very likely."

"Should we warn her?" I asked. My aunts were seldom wrong, and I began to think that it would be our duty to forewarn Annabelle Heskitt.

"I don't think that would be wise."

Murmurs of agreement passed between my aunts.

"If Annabelle is as besotted with her fellow as Mrs. Driscoll tells us she is, then we shouldn't interfere."

"And besides, Annabelle is already a wealthy woman so has already prospered. The curse in that case is redundant."

"Hmm, I guess," I said.

"Anyway, dear. It's really none of our business. It is between the Heskitts and whoever cursed them."

"Exactly."

"Indeed."

As usual, I was left with more questions at the end of the conversation than I had at the beginning. I definitely wanted to know who had cursed the Heskitts and, if they weren't alive, just how the curse could be broken.

As my aunts murmured their agreement, my thoughts began to drift to Garrett and the Blackwood curse until a sprinkle of white dust fell from the ceiling and spattered the table.

Chapter Three

"Ugh!" Aunt Euphemia complained. "There's dust in my tea!"

"It came from the ceiling."

Above Aunt Euphemia, between the beams, a crack had appeared in the plaster. The paint, ordinarily a bright white, had yellowed and begun to flake.

"The whole place is falling apart!" Aunt Beatrice exclaimed as more dust fell. She removed the spoiled cup of tea, brushing at the dust on the table.

"The front door is stiff too," I added as I watched sprinkles of paint drift downwards. "I struggled to pull it open this morning."

Aunt Euphemia stepped away from the falling particles. "We *have* to make discovering who is attacking Haligern a priority. And before the cottage crumbles to the ground!"

"I was up all night, reading through my book," Aunt Thomasin said with a weary sigh. "I'm not sure what else I can do."

Beside Aunt Loveday, with his head resting on massive paws, Renweard became alert, stared across the room, and growled.

I followed his gaze to the chimney breast. Dust sprinkled from the gap in the broken mantel. From high within the chimney came the sound of grating. Renweard jumped forward, barking at the noise, hackles raised.

"It's alright," I soothed. "Just a few bricks coming loose." My words were an empty gesture that brought no comfort as the grating continued. If the noise were bricks coming loose then the entire chimney could collapse! In the next moment my concern for the chimney evaporated as I heard a pain-filled gasp. I turned to see Uncle Raif clasping his chest!

In the next second the grating became a rumble and the kitchen filled with the thud and crash of bricks as the flue collapsed into the hearth. A cloud of soot and ash billowed from the fireplace. Renweard growled, ran to the chimney, barked at the falling stones, then returned to Aunt Loveday's side. She swayed, unsteady on her feet, then staggered.

Realising that she was about to crash to the floor, I leapt forward, catching her just as her legs gave way. Still seated, Uncle Raif gasped for breath, his face pulled into a grimace of pain. In my arms, Aunt Loveday's frame was bird-like and fragile. In that moment, a horrifying realisation struck me; they were dying!

As the rumbling subsided, the pain on Uncle Raif's face eased and he managed a relieved groan. With Aunt Thomasin's help, I sat Aunt Loveday beside him. With both more comfortable, I opened the door to allow the breeze to attack the clouded air. I pictured the black particles being swept up and out of the room in a cleansing vortex, and the soot and ash eddied then disappeared through the open doorway.

A final stone tumbled down the chimney, dropped into the ashes, and rolled out onto the stone hearth. Smoke seeped from the crack in the chimney breast. Now completely broken, it would have to be repaired before we were able to light a warming fire. My energy sagged as I realised that, at this rate, the house would be derelict within weeks.

As the dust settled, and distressed chatter quietened. Aunts Beatrice, Euphemia, and Thomasin hovered close to Raif and Loveday. Both appeared fatigued, but at least free from pain. Loveday held Raif's hand, her eyes filled with concern.

"Uncle Raif, are you alright?" I asked. He was far from alright, but I needed to hear him say that he was.

He nodded and offered a weak, "Yes, dear. You mustn't worry. I'm just an old man."

I wasn't convinced. "We should call Dr. Cotta-"

"Please don't worry," he insisted. "It's just a momentary thing. The pain will pass."

"Calling the doctor won't help, Livitha," Aunt Euphemia stated.

I was surprised at how matter of fact she was. "But if he's in pain, surely we must call a doctor or take him to hospital!"

"Please don't worry, Livitha," Uncle Raif repeated. "Your aunt is all I need." He stroked Loveday's hand.

"But Dr. Cotta-"

"There is nothing earthly medicine can do for him." Aunt Loveday cast a pain-filled glance at her husband. "Raif is unwell because of me. It is my magick that is at fault."

Uncle Raif shook his head. "Now, now, Loveday, that is simply not true."

"Not at all," Aunt Euphemia agreed. "Your magick-"

"My magick is not strong enough-"

"Then we must make it strong again!" I said, unable to take my eyes from Uncle Raif. "We must find out who or what is attacking Haligern and stop them!" Desperation seeped from every cell in my body. I expected Aunt Loveday to meet my own determination with her own, but she seemed infused with apathy. Impossibly, her aura was dulled and leaked a hopeless energy. This was not the Aunt Loveday I knew. I looked to my aunts for guidance and suddenly, the situation became clear.

"The hex," I said, "it's not directed at Haligern."

Five pairs of eyes watched me with varying degrees of confusion.

"It's not Haligern!" I repeated. "It's so obvious now. Each time the house has aged, so has Uncle Raif and now Aunt Loveday is ageing too. Her deterioration hasn't been so obvious because she was stronger than Uncle Raif, and it was *her* magick that was keeping him alive." That my other aunts had remained unaffected was the key to my hypothesis. I swung to them. "You are all still healthy! You haven't aged at all!"

"Livitha, you're getting a little overexcited."

Loveday raised a weak hand. "Let her speak."

"All this time we've been looking for a way to protect Haligern, but all the time it was Loveday who was being attacked." I took Aunt Thomasin by the shoulders and twisted her to the small mirror on the wall, its silver was now pitted with grey spots. "Look! You haven't aged at all. All these weeks that Uncle Raif has been sick, you've been fine."

"Well ... it's terrible that Raif is unwell, but I can't help being healthy, Livitha!" She said this with an air of desperation. "I wish it were me that was sick and not Raif!"

"No, that's not what I mean."

"What do you mean?"

"That the curse, or hex, or whatever it is, is only directed at Loveday. She is being poisoned!" I twirled to her now, taking in the thinness of her skin and rheumy eyes.

As I caught her gaze, she nodded. "I think the child is right. I do feel terrible. I've fought it for weeks now, but it is winning."

"I suppose Livitha could be right."

"I am! You're being poisoned and because it's your magick that is keeping Uncle Raif alive and the cottage pristine, they're deteriorating with you."

"Goodness!" blurted Aunt Beatrice. "She is right! Why didn't we see it?"

"Because we've all been so worried about Uncle Raif—he has suffered most, until now."

"Oh, dear. Whatever shall we do?"

"Well, now that we know that it is Loveday who is being attacked, we can find out who it is. It has to be an enemy!"

"An enemy! But who would hate us this much?"

"I can think of several," Aunt Loveday said, her voice a rasp.

"Then you must tell me!"

"Oh, Livitha, I'm not sure I have the energy left."

I swallowed back tears. My emotions were becoming unstable and watching two of the people I loved most in the world hurtling towards their final days, was unbearable. I had to discover a cure! "You do!" I blurted. "You do and I'm going to find them and stop them and save you both!"

She managed a wan smile.

"That's my girl!" Uncle Raif managed.

Chapter Four

Weak and tired, Aunt Loveday hadn't been able to come up with the names of any enemies with a credible motive for hurting her and, after ten minutes, it had become obvious that she needed to rest, as did Uncle Raif. With my aunts caring for the pair, and a variety of spells being cast to shore up the positive energy in the house, it had been decided that I should continue the day as normal and open the shop. Apart from worry, there was very little I could do at home, so I agreed. Plus, the quieter, less fractious energy there would allow me to think more clearly.

One of the features of the shop that Mike the builder had helped to restore was a fireplace and we had opted to install a small wood burner to help warm the rooms. This morning I was glad of it, as a chill wind had begun to blow through the village. As I lit the kindling, golden leaves eddied outside the window.

As the firewood began to burn, I made myself a coffee, allowing my thoughts to whir and cogitate. Since my initiation, my aunts had been able to speak more freely about their past and there were numerous peculiar, often hilarious, incidents that they could now relate from a history that spanned centuries. Some stories were a little darker than others and it was obvious that my aunts were not averse to using their magical powers to overcome people who presented a challenge. Often their magick was used to serve justice, or stop an injustice, but had it ever been used to cause harm?

As my curiosity grew, so did my understanding of the depth of their powers and knowledge, and the previous night I had stayed up until the early hours, poring through Arthur, Aunt Loveday's spell and history-filled grimoire, in the hope that it would somehow give me answers or even some clue as to what may be happening at the house. Unable to bring Arthur with me to the shop, I sat behind the counter, notebook open, pen in hand, and waited for my thoughts to begin firing. Although I hadn't been searching for enemies through his pages, I felt sure that something I had read during those hours would help me understand who could be harming her—if only I could connect the dots.

Coffee steamed from the cup beside me as I searched my memories of the night's reading. One thing was certain, Aunt Loveday's past was far darker than I had known. Among the charms for gathering herbs and shrinking cysts, there were spells for the defeat of foes, cursing dwarves, and the destruction of an enemy. I had also found three recipes for creating poppets and precise instructions for causing harm to the intended victim.

It struck me that there were so many things in our lives that were not what they appeared to be. Old Mawde for example, the nanny goat that was not a goat, but a woman cursed by Loveday centuries ago. The cursed creature had been supplying us with milk on a daily basis for years!

My mind returned to Aunt Loveday's affliction—the sapping of her magical strength that was causing her to age rapidly.

Unnoticed, she had slowly deteriorated over a period of weeks as though she were being poisoned!

Poison!

What if it was a physical rather than metaphysical poison? Not a curse, but something she had eaten, or had touched? I mulled this hypothesis over for some minutes. If it were a chemical poison, then that person had to have access to Loveday and the only person who had regular access was Mrs. Driscoll. That suggestion was simply ridiculous. Wasn't it? I dismissed the idea. It had to be a curse, someone working from a distance. I made numerous curling doodles on my pad as I mulled over the problem but got no further. Frustrated by my lack of knowledge but determined to learn more about curses - I would become the foremost expert! - I took the last sip of coffee and filled the last white space on my pad with another curling, flowery doodle. Aunt Loveday had an enemy, but I still had no idea where to start my investigation. As I drummed my finger on the counter, the bell tinkled, and Mrs. Driscoll walked through the door. Behind her was another customer. I forced a smile as they entered.

"Morning, Liv!" Mrs. Driscoll's voice had a distinctly happy lilt.

Discomfort at my thoughts pricked me. It was unthinkable that the saintly Mrs. Driscoll would poison my aunt. I pushed the disloyal thought away and forced myself to focus. "Good morning, Mrs. Driscoll! It's lovely to see you here."

The other lady hovered by Mrs. Driscoll's side and then wandered across the shop to the large dresser. Vintage and locally made pestle and mortar sets sat beside Aunt Thomasin's hand-carved and moon-magic infused rune sets. She took a mugwort and sage cleansing stick from a large glass jar.

"Well, it's such a lovely morning that I thought we'd take a stroll and then I remembered that it's my niece's birthday next week. I've come in for some of that lovely lotion I bought last week. I know she'll love it too. And I've got a terrible blister on my heel. Do you have anything for that?"

"I'm sure we do." I retrieved our best-selling anti-ageing cream and a herbal balm that would soothe her damaged skin and placed them on the counter. "Is there anything else I can help you with?"

The younger woman placed the items she had selected on the counter.

"Oh, Liv, let me introduce you to my friend." A beatific smile lifted Mrs. Driscoll's face as she glanced at the woman.

"Liv, this is Lina."

A pair of dark blue eyes, irises edged with midnight, flickering with curiosity, and framed with thick black lashes, held me in their gaze. An abundance of dark and glossy curls surrounded her face, falling onto her shoulders. Free of make-up, apart from a slight gloss to her full lips, her skin had the glow of wrinkle-free youth and there wasn't a single hint of wayward hairs or sagging jawline. Slightly shorter than Mrs. Driscoll, Lina was petite and extremely pretty. With her dewy skin she had the glamour of youth, but the maturity of a woman of at least forty. I could see why Mrs. Driscoll seemed so thrilled to introduce her but, more than her appearance, it was her aura that caught my attention. Obscured as though I were viewing it through opaque glass, the glimmering fragments I could see were cerise. I had never seen anything like it. As her energy vibrated, I felt immediately drawn to her.

"It's lovely to meet you, Liv." Like her appearance, her smile with its perfectly white and beautifully aligned teeth, was alluring. Her voice was soft and silky. Her eyes shone with the promise of friendship.

"And you," I replied. "I haven't seen you in the village before. Are you a local?" I asked, curious about her now.

"No, I've just moved into the village."

"She's taken Foxglove Cottage."

I knew the cottage. It sat just outside of the village and was picture perfect with a thatched roof at the centre of a large garden entered through a rose-laden archway. It did however have a reputation. I glanced at the cleansing stick on the table wondering if Lina was already experiencing trouble. "It's a beautiful place," I enthused. "How are you finding it?" Despite its charmingly bucolic name, Foxglove Cottage was one of those houses that would pass through numerous hands until the right owner came along. There had never been any talk of 'spirits' associated with it, but it was just one of those homes that seemed to run through a spate of owners until it settled on the one it liked. That was my opinion anyway. Pascal had told me my ideas about houses were a 'load of old rubbish,' but I knew it was true. Every town has some; the houses that keep cropping up for sale.

"I absolutely love it!" she enthused. "It has so much character and charm. I can't wait until summer. The garden will be stunning."

This was good news. Perhaps the cottage had found its forever owner?

"It was overgrown when you moved in, but you've made a start haven't you," Mrs. Driscoll added. "She loves to garden."

Lina nodded and smiled. "I do," she agreed.

"Me too!" I said remembering the beautiful garden I had created at my home with Pascal. Haligern's gardens were beautiful too, and I found them a solace for my loss.

"I don't know where I'd be without my garden. It fills me with such good energy to be out in nature."

"I know exactly what you mean!" I empathised. "If I'm feeling a little antsy, a walk in the garden blows that horrible energy away."

"It does!" She threw me a smile of mutual recognition.

Several minutes passed as we talked about our love of flowers and gardening and the soothing, therapeutic properties of being in nature.

"I particularly love walking through the woods. It's one of the reasons I moved here," she said. "There are so many ancient woodlands in this part of the country."

"We are lucky," I agreed. There were at least three areas of dense woodland; Haligern, the Black Woods, and those that surrounded the Heskitt estate.

As we continued to chat, Mrs. Driscoll's smile dropped, and a small crease appeared between her brows as her energy changed. She locked her eyes on me, her lips narrowing to a disapproving line. Realising that she was staring, I glanced at her then quickly looked away. Talking with Lina was invigorating but the uncharacteristic change in Mrs. Driscoll was making me uncomfortable. I turned the conversation to the items on the counter, wrapped the women's purchases, and took their money. With the focus back on herself, Mrs. Driscoll's irritated energy waned and was replaced by a genuine smile, particularly when she had Lina's attention. After several minutes they said their goodbyes and left the shop.

I watched them leave with surprised elation; talking to Lina had been great and I knew she was someone I could be friends with. Since discovering I was a witch, I had reduced the amount of time I spent with my friends and was feeling a little lonely on that score. However, if we were to be friends, I would have to deal with Mrs. Driscoll's strangely intense jealousy.

Spats between friends were something I had always sought to avoid, but in that moment, I felt that winning Lina's friendship, even if it did mean falling out with Mrs. Driscoll, would be worth it. As they disappeared from view, my thoughts returned to Aunt Loveday and the fact that she was being poisoned. That Mrs. Driscoll could be a suspect didn't seem so ridiculous now!

Chapter Five

The following day, I came down to breakfast to a busy kitchen. The fire, now unusable, remained unlit, but the spells and charms that my aunts had cast the day before were obviously doing some good as Aunt Loveday had managed to get dressed and leave her room. After yesterday's drama I had expected her to have deteriorated even more.

Aunt Beatrice filled the kettle to make a pot of tea whilst Aunts Euphemia, Thomasin, and Loveday sat at the table, each with a grimoire opened before her, each with their head bent low and studying its pages. Aunt Loveday was pallid and frail, but obviously feeling well enough to pore over Arthur. Aunt Thomasin held a magnifying glass to her grimoire, hovering over tiny symbols written along the edge of a page filled with illustrations and text. Unlike her 'modern' hand, this text was not written in a beautiful copperplate script. She huffed. "If only I'd written it a little larger, sisters! I can barely read it, particularly where it has faded."

I hovered to look, fascinated by their books. Each one was ancient, a collection of spells, charms, and hexes, collected over centuries. The first parchment leaves of Arthur, Aunt Loveday's grimoire, dated from the eighth century when she had begun to record her knowledge. Each book was a testament to their courage, tomes of forbidden knowledge kept safe throughout the centuries when witchcraft was frowned upon and punished. Given the fear and suspicion with which witches were regarded, it was a miracle that the books, and my aunts, had survived this long. Their histories, which they loved to remind each other of during long evenings in front of the fire, were peppered with memories of friends who had lost their lives to persecution and the bonfires, or 'bone fires' as my aunts called them, another linguistic relic of their long-lived lives.

Aunt Beatrice placed a large teapot in the middle of the table and removed the cups and saucers used earlier in the morning. I took my place at the table. My aunts continued to study their grimoires, scanning one page and then another. I poured myself a cup of tea and thanked Aunt Beatrice for the freshly baked bread roll placed on a plate in front of me.

Lucifer lay curled with Bess to one side of the hearth and Renweard lay at Aunt Loveday's feet. The air vibrated with anticipation and restrained energy. I yearned to fling the door open and let the sun's rays cleanse the room of this pent-up energy but, like yesterday, the sun was muted behind a bank of fog.

With my breakfast finished, I helped Aunt Beatrice to dry the washed pots.

"I want to help, but what can I do?" I asked as I dried the cup favoured by Aunt Loveday, a finely shaped bone china teacup decorated with hand-painted flowers and edged with gold that dated from the late nineteenth century. I reached for its matching saucer.

"They're doing their best to find a solution. It will come. We have to remain steady. Panicking will only weaken Loveday further."

I sighed, frustrated. There had to be something more we could do other than just pore through books!

"They hold so much knowledge, Livitha," Aunt Beatrice said quietly. "We must trust in their power."

Aunt Beatrice had read my mind again, but I was too concerned about the hex to reprimand her.

"It's just that I feel so useless! I have nothing to offer."

"Of course you do. When the time is right, we will discover how to use our magick against it."

As though on cue, Aunt Thomasin yelped. "I have it!"

Aunt Euphemia rose to look at Thomasin's grimoire. Aunt Loveday peered across the table. Startled, Bess jumped up and Lucifer hissed before closing his eyes.

"What have you found?"

"It is a hex against a hex! To create a shield within a shield."

"Why didn't I think of that!" Aunt Loveday's voice was filled with recrimination.

"You have been so concerned about Raif, dear sister, and this hex is taking its toll upon you too." Aunt Thomasin slid a hand over Aunt Loveday's and offered a loving smile.

"But I should have!" Tears welled in her eyes. "It is such a simple thing, really, but I just did not think of it. Oh, sisters, what is happening? I can barely think for the muddiness inside my mind." Aunt Loveday's voice had acquired an aged tone, and she stroked her throat with fingers that were increasingly gnarled.

"Stay quiet, sister," Aunt Euphemia said in soothing tones. "Let us carry this burden."

"Yes, Loveday. This time it is we who must work. You cannot carry everything upon your shoulders."

Aunt Loveday made a nod of acceptance and blotted a tear from her cheek. "You're right."

Murmured agreement filled the kitchen.

Suddenly agitated, Aunt Loveday asked, "Has Raif returned?"

"Returned, dear?"

"He hasn't been out, surely?"

"Has he returned from Kedleston? I told him it was dangerous."

My aunts exchanged confused glances. Weak with age, Uncle Raif hadn't left the house for several weeks now.

"Has he returned?"

"I think so?" offered Aunt Euphemia.

"He promised to bring me some seeds of woad."

Concerned glances were shared among the sisters and I felt the pit of my stomach turn.

"Yes, dear. He has returned." Aunt Beatrice's voice was laced with sadness. "Why don't you join him? He's in the sitting room. I can bring you both a nice cup of tea. You must be tired after all your hard work."

"Yes, I do feel tired, Beatrice."

"Thomasin will walk with you," she said with a nod to my aunt. "I'll send the tea through with Livitha."

With Aunt Loveday settled in the sitting room with Uncle Raif, both warm in front of the fire, the room filled with concerned chatter.

"What on earth is going on?"

"She is ageing. She was experiencing the past."

"They call it Alzheimers, I think."

"Just as Raif did the other week?"

"Yes, exactly that."

Several weeks ago, Uncle Raif had experienced some confusion and imagined that he was back in Tudor England, a young man again.

"So, do you think that Uncle Raif's illness was the first sign of the hex?" I asked. "That's when his health began to decline and that's when Aunt Loveday's energy began to change," I said. "At least, when I think back, that's when I noticed it. I put the changes down to her worry about Uncle Raif, but now I think that this dark magick has been poisoning her for weeks!"

Aunt Euphemia nodded. "I think you're right, Liv."

"So, is that a good thing?"

"A good thing!"

"What I mean is, if the hex is taking this long to work, then perhaps the person who cast it isn't as powerful as we think?"

"Hmm! It's a thought, but I'm not sure. Some hexes are slow to work, and this one has begun as a seed and is increasing in power. At least that is how it seems."

"She's right, Liv. Some hexes only grow in power rather than erupt as a burst of evil."

"So that it's taking time isn't a sign that the person is an amateur?"

Aunt Thomasin shook her head. "Sadly, I think it could mean quite the opposite. It is an insidious hex that only makes itself known over time and once it has had a chance to grow long and tenacious roots."

I shuddered.

"Our best hope, until something else comes to light, is the shield spell Aunt Thomasin found."

"Do you think the spell will work?"

"We have to try. What is harming Loveday is a powerful hex, and I have only used this shield spell once, and that was many centuries ago, when-"

A rap at the back door was followed by a tapping at the window as Benny, Thomasin's raven, demanded to be let in. He seemed flustered and flapped his wings before tapping at the window again.

Ordinarily, Benny would hop through the door then jump up onto a chair, but this morning he swooped through the open door and flapped about the room before landing on the table. In his beak was an object which he dropped beside Thomasin's grimoire.

"Whatever is wrong, Ben-" Thomasin's flow of words came to an abrupt halt.

Aunt Beatrice hissed and Aunt Euphemia took a sharp intake of breath.

I stepped forward to get a better look at the object.

"Don't touch it!" Aunt Thomasin said spreading her arms as a barrier. "Get back!"

"I'll get it," Aunt Beatrice said with a decisive tone threaded with anger.

With hand encased in a large oven mitt, she hooked the item with a metal skewer and held it at arms-length.

"What is it?" I asked peering at the object now held aloft. Obviously handmade, the object appeared mundane, a twisted knot of twigs and rags threaded with sprays of berries. There was also what looked like a small bone tied to it.

"Weasel bones and black bryony."

"It is a geunlybba wealsáda. A poison tether. It binds dark magick to its victim." Aunt Thomasin's face was grim, the flicker of fear replaced by a stony anger. "Benny, where did you find this?"

Aunt Euphemia stared at the object, flinching as Beatrice stepped passed her as she walked towards the door. "It was brave of him to bring it to us."

"No!" Aunt Thomasin snapped. "It was foolish. He could have been hurt."

Benny chirruped angrily then hopped onto her shoulder before whispering into her ear.

"I know, Benny, but you must not take such risks. Where did you find it?"

He spoke into her ear, chirruped, then hopped back down to the table.

"Sisters, make yourselves ready. Benny is going to take us to the place he found it."

"Where?"

"In the woods, close to the woodsman's cottage."

"On Haligern land?"

"Yes," she said with a hiss. "On Haligern land."

Chapter Six

We were ready to follow Benny within five minutes and, with coats buttoned and the laces of our walking boots tied, we marched across the lawn, past the vegetable garden and then across the meadow to the forest. Thick fog obscured the distant trees but, as we continued to tramp across the recently mowed meadow, our boots quickly becoming wet with the morning dew, it thinned to patchy, then cleared enough for us to see ahead.

Benny flew above, circling and swooping to allow us to catch up, repeatedly alighting upon Aunt Thomasin's shoulder before taking off again.

"He is terribly overexcited," Aunt Thomasin exclaimed as Benny launched himself once more from her shoulder. "I can barely understand what he's saying. I think finding the tether has caused him a great deal of consternation."

"He was lucky the geunlybba wealsáda didn't carry a deáþbérnis hex too!"

"Indeed! That's an old trick."

"What exactly is a deathbernis hex?" I asked catching my breath. With Aunt Thomasin striding ahead as she followed Benny, we were walking at quite a pace. At times, I had to nearly run to keep up with the others. It was obvious, though the youngest of the women, I was the least fit. It was a situation I had to remedy, along with the extra rolls of fat that still clung to my waistline like magnetic pool noodles!

An enviously slender Aunt Euphemia strode beside me, her cheeks ruddy from effort. Walking beside her, arms pumping, was Aunt Beatrice. Deceptively strong and sprightly, she showed little sign of the struggle I was experiencing. Although they presented as elderly women, they were in good health and strong. I had gained my magical powers but was still overweight and menopausal. Why? It was an issue I had to resolve; there was no way I could face going through centuries being overweight and menopausal!

"It is a protective spell," Aunt Thomasin explained, "But of the dark magick variety."

"That makes it sound really rather innocuous, Thomasin," Aunt Euphemia countered. "It's far more dreadful. It is a death-bringing hex, and one that can be cast over an object. It's not unheard of for a witch-"

"Or wizard."

"Yes, or wizard - thank you Beatrice – to cast a spell that gives a shock-"

"Or causes death."

"Yes, or causes death, to the person who finds it and picks it up."

"And sometimes they're laced with physical poison!" Aunt Beatrice said with authority, her eyes squinting, and lips pursed in disapproval. "So, if you touch it you die!" she finished with dramatic flair.

"Which is why we were so careful when Benny dropped it onto the table."

"And why Thomasin is so cross with him."

"And is so relieved that he has shown no ill-effects."

"Precisely."

"It does have to be said," continued Aunt Beatrice, "That it really is a very useful spell." She huffed as she strode, almost trotting by Aunt Euphemia's side.

"Well, it's certainly poisonous!"

"It is, and so, is a great deterrent. Do you remember Selma Meldrake?"

Aunt Euphemia pulled a frown as she searched her memories. Her breath puffed in white clouds and her cheeks were flushed with the effort of walking so fast, but the colour only served to enhance her beauty. I, on the other hand, had sweat beginning to trickle down my back and probably looked blotchy and flustered.

"I'm not sure that I do. Remind me."

"Oh, Euphemia! You must! Selma Meldrake," she repeated. She lived in the village before moving up north. In the Old Forge on West Street. Do you remember that she was being pursued by Percy Wharram, the Tax Collector?"

"Oh, yes! Of course. He was besotted, but far too old for her."

"That's right, he had already buried two wives but managed to persuade Selma's mother that they should marry."

"Bribed her more like."

"I think there were threats made to the poor widow, Percy was not a man to be refused! Anyway, Selma used the spell to repulse Percy. So, each time they met she wore a tether and each time being around her made him feel unwell. Eventually he called off the wedding."

Aunt Beatrice cackled. "She grew to be a wily old crone. Ah! It would be good to see her again. Do you think she will be at *The Gathering*?"

"It's possible."

I listened to their story with interest; there were numerous depths to my aunts and, as I had discovered over the past few days, they hadn't lived lives of sugar and spice and all things nice. There were definitely a few slugs, snails, and puppy dogs' tails in the brew too.

We broke through a patch of thick fog to see Aunt Thomasin step into the forest and Benny swoop to follow.

"Thomasin!" Aunt Beatrice called. "Wait for us!"

"We should have flown," Aunt Euphemia complained as we all picked up the pace. "My feet are sodden!"

"Not during daylight, dear. You know the rules."

Aunt Euphemia harumphed. "Sometimes, I am quite sick of the 'rules' Beatrice!"

Moments later, with Haligern Cottage hidden in the fog behind us, we stood before a bank of trees. Without the sun, the forest seemed dark and ominous, and I was relieved when Aunt Thomasin announced that it was not necessary to go very deep into the woods as we were close to the place Benny had found the poison tether. Benny squawked, chittered into her ear, then sidestepped to nuzzle close to her head.

"Follow me."

We followed Aunt Thomasin, guided by Benny, until the reason for his excitement became horribly clear.

Standing in a small clearing was a wooden structure of three posts. At the top of the structure, each post was attached by coils of rope to a crossbeam. The crossbeams formed a horizontal triangle from which, hung by their feet, were at least a dozen, obviously dead, ravens. Benny quivered and squawked at the structure then flew from Aunt Thomasin's shoulder, disappearing through the forest and back out into the clearing.

"Poor Benny!" gasped Aunt Beatrice. "I'm not surprised he was so excited."

"He's in shock. Terrified!"

I took a step closer. Each bird had its feet tied together and its beak wrapped with twine. "This is awful!" I declared. "Who would do this?"

"Whoever is attacking Loveday. That's who," Aunt Beatrice said with conviction. "Someone who is practising a dark, dark magick. I have not seen one of these for many centuries."

"They are quite arcane, even for us witches."

"But what is it?" I asked staring up at the structure. It was at least eight feet high.

"It is a forlædan deáþbeám, a death-bringing gallows. An offering shrine for the darkest of evil forces. The witch stands in the middle and, surrounded by death, conjures dark magick to do her bidding."

"So, the witch that built this, stood here whilst she hexed Loveday?"

"I am certain of that. Being close to the victim is efficacious to the hex—it oils the cogs, as they say."

I scoured the area looking for signs of anyone lurking then turned my attention to the base of the gallows-like structure. At its centre, the earth was scuffed, the leaves and twigs of the forest floor broken and torn, the earth turned; evidence of the witch's movement as she worked. The area surrounding the structure was also trodden down and a pathway obvious through the undergrowth. "Well, whoever did it, made no effort to cover their tracks." I crouched to examine the foliage. Some had been crushed underfoot and had withered, whilst other leaves and stems were broken but still green and fleshy. "And they've been here more than once. Quite recently too." The trail of evidence led away from the structure. "You can see where they've walked through the forest." I pointed out the track and then retraced the witch's footsteps, sure that I would find more clues but, after about ten feet, I was surrounded by undamaged foliage. "Where did she go? I can't see which way. The trail ends here."

"That confirms it sisters," Aunt Euphemia said. "If the trail ends here, it can mean only one thing."

"Or two."

"Yes, Beatrice, or two."

"Go on?" I urged.

"Well, they had the power of flight-"

"Or spondition."

"Yes, or spondition. Thank you, Beatrice."

I had never heard of the word. To my ears it sounded odd. "And what exactly is 'spondition'?"

"It's our word for 'spontaneous intra-dimensional transportation,'" Aunt Beatrice explained. "Oh, and inter-dimensional transportation."

It *was* a terrible word! I frowned, no closer to understanding.

"It is the ability to move from one place to another in an instant, the stepping out of this dimension and into another only to reappear in a different position in the first dimension only seconds later. We can walk within and between dimensions."

"So, kind of like they do in Star Trek?"

"Yes, if you like, like Star Trek, but without the funny noises or console. It takes magick only, but it takes a powerful and knowledgeable witch to achieve it."

"Sisters, we are dealing with a terrible foe!"

"Indeed we are, Beatrice."

"And on Haligern land!"

"The audacity is reprehensible."

"Ruthless!"

"Criminal!"

"Come," said Aunt Thomasin with authority. "We have much work to do, sisters."

Chapter Seven

Back at the cottage, we gathered in the drawing room where Aunt Loveday sat, blanket across her knees, beside the fire. Obviously snoozing, she woke only after Aunt Beatrice had given her shoulder a gentle prod.

"Oh! I must have dozed off."

"That's understandable, dear," soothed Aunt Beatrice.

A flicker of fear passed over Aunt Loveday's face before she managed a welcoming smile.

Watching her struggle made me impatient and I took control of the conversation. "We found it!"

"What did you find?"

"The gallows. The poison that's harming you."

At this, she perked up, pulling herself straight in the armchair, drawing on her dwindling energy to become alert. "Tell me!"

"It's a ... what did you call it Aunt Thomasin? A death tree?"

"We found a death-bringing tree, Loveday."

Aunt Loveday's eyes narrowed, and her brow became furrowed. "A forlǽdan deáþbeám! This is serious."

"It's murder Loveday!" Aunt Beatrice hissed. "Murder!"

"Be calm, sister. I must think clearly, and my energy is low, my mind so fuddled!"

Although the energy in the room remained fractious, we waited with as much calm as we could muster as Loveday leant back in the chair. With eyes closed, she said, "The death-bringing gallows is a conductor of dark magick. It is the source of the hex. Did you find the circle of tethers?"

"There are more?"

"Yes, they will have been placed to encircle the house."

"We didn't look," I admitted.

"If the witch is using the death-bringing gallows to attack me, then the poison tether Benny found is likely to be one of many that rings the house. All must be collected and then doused before their poisonous energy can be damped."

"We have to go back then," I said, ready to head back to the woods.

Aunt Loveday nodded. "Yes, I'm afraid you will. Collect them all—they will be connected with string, or twine, so easy to find, but you must be careful not to touch them. When you return, we will have a good bone fire."

"What about the gallows?"

"Break it apart and bring it here. We shall have to burn that too."

The gallows wasn't a massive structure, nor had it been constructed to be robust, so it would be easy to break apart and bring back to Haligern.

"Let's go then," I said, eager to begin the job and break the poisonous energy that was causing us so much damage.

"One minute, Livitha. You must collect the items carefully," Loveday warned. "Euphemia, you are to cast a charm of protection around you all, but each of you must recite a dilution charm as you pick up the poison tethers up." The exertion of talking had made her breathless and she remained quiet as she took several restorative breaths. "Beatrice, please bring Arthur to me."

Loveday began to leaf through his pages until finally stopping and pointing a bony finger at lines written in dark ink. "Here it is. These are the words you must recite. Commit them to memory, Livitha." She looked up from the book. "And when you return, write them down. They are to be added to your own grimoire."

"Very generous, Loveday," Aunt Euphemia said.

"My own grimoire!"

"Yes, Livitha. So much has occurred since your fiftieth birthday that your instruction in our magick has been lacking, but once this emergency is over, we must begin. In the meantime, you can begin to collect spells and charms-"

"And hexes!"

"Yes, and hexes. Thank you, Beatrice."

"It's so exciting!"

Aunt Loveday smiled. "It is, dear sister, and we will begin instruction after this foe has been defeated."

"And we will defeat them. As we have done in the past."

Murmured agreement passed between my aunts.

"They will regret trying to harm the witches of Haligern coven!"

Aunt Beatrice cackled. "And I know just the punishment."

"Sisters! Let us focus," reprimanded Aunt Loveday as the conversation turned to the revenge that would be taken against this newest enemy. I can't deny that I wasn't a little disappointed. Revenge was something I wanted too and some of my aunts' ideas were fascinating.

"Now listen and learn, Livitha, daughter of Soren." Sitting with a straight back, her hands laid across Arthur's open pages, eyes closed, she began to recite ancient words.

Focusing on the flow of sound, I absorbed the words, elated as the magick welded itself to my memory. It was a strange sensation. Generally, I struggled to recall memories, but knew, without doubt, that the ancient words were being passed over, and recorded in my mind, forever. "I'm ready," I said as Aunt Loveday grew quiet.

"Then let's return to the forest," urged Aunt Thomasin.

With the charm repeating in my mind, and armed with gardening gloves, buckets, and a length of rope, I walked back to the death-bringing gallows with Aunt Thomasin. Given the strength of the poisonous hex, Aunts Beatrice and Euphemia had stayed behind to shore up the shield of positive, health-giving energy that protected Aunt Loveday and Uncle Raif.

Until today walking through Haligern's woodland had been a pleasure, joyous even. I loved to walk beneath its canopy, run my hand across the bark of its ancient trees. Dappled light would fall across the forest floor illuminating the emerald-green ferns, lighting the mounds of moss. Everything delighted me, from the clusters of rust-coloured fungus and creamy toadstools to the native foxgloves that appeared like brilliant gems. Returning to the forest this morning however, I was filled with dread determination and not a little anger. How dare another witch attack my aunt. How very dare they!

We made our way directly to the Tyburn-like death tree. By this time, my anger had swelled. The heat at my core was rising and the tingling in my fingers was becoming unbearable. I did little to repress it, enjoying the sense of growing power. When this increase in raw magick had happened in the past, it had filled me with panic. This time I knew exactly what to do with the barely controllable energy.

At twenty feet from the death tree, I instructed Aunt Thomasin to stand back and, before she had a chance to object, unleashed the fizzing at my fingertips and threw the sparkling energy at the death-bringing gallows. Super-charged magick blew like a bolt of lightning from my fingertips—and missed.

"Liv!" Aunt Thomasin shouted as a tree beyond the gallows exploded, splintering the forest with charred wood. "What are you doing?"

Blown back by the force, I stumbled to a fall, landing heavily on my backside, grunting as the wind was knocked out of me. With pain spreading like a tidal wave through my coccyx, I could only stare at the devastation. It had been a powerful blast, but I had messed up. "Damn!"

Helping hand outstretched, Aunt Thomasin shook her head with exasperated disapproval. "Liv, whatever were you thinking?"

"I wanted to blast it. I hate it so much!" Overcome by emotion, tears began to flow and rose to a sob. "I'm sorry!" I said, "I let my emotions get the better of me." I took her hand. "Just ignore me. Must be the hormones."

"It's understandable, dear," she said, helping me to my feet, "but we must do this in a calm and collected manner. Your hormones will just have to behave!"

I sighed.

"Don't worry, Liv. I do understand," she said with kindness. "It's something you'll learn over time, but today you must try your utmost to reign in your anger and need for vengeance. The old saying is true, 'revenge is a dish best served cold'!"

"Well," I said, my voice still unsteady with emotion. "I shall serve it with a slice of Haligern wrath!"

"That's my girl! Now, let's start again."

Chapter Eight

We stood together surveying the damaged tree, thankful it hadn't burst into flame, then checked for any stray embers that might ignite. Once satisfied the forest wasn't about to burn to the ground, we turned our attention to the death-bringing tree.

"Aunt Loveday said that there will be a linked circle of geunlybba wealsáda. I guess we should find the beginning and work our way around." I was pleased with how easily the ancient name for the poison tether had slipped from my tongue.

"Nicely pronounced, dear," Aunt Thomasin said with a smile of approval and then sighed. "I hope the witch has been lazy and placed them around the inner woodland perimeter!"

We decided that once we had found the twine that held the poison tethers, we would each follow an end and meet in the middle. Plan formulated, and gloved hands gripping bucket handles, we stepped close to the death-bringing tree and began our search for the twine. It was easy to find. Brushing away the piles of leaves heaped around its posts, revealed that string had been tied to two of them. For several feet, the string had been covered over with leaves and twigs but then left to lay unhidden. With string untied from the post, I pulled. Leaves and twigs fell away as the string rose to reveal the first poison tether. As before, it was a circular object of woven twigs, bones, and fabric.

"I have one!" I called. I recited the charm as I snipped the string either side then grasped it with a pair of fireside tongs before holding it up to the light. Twigs had been woven into a circle with a piece of fabric, the same fabric that had been on the object Benny had brought back to the cottage. Entwined with the twigs and fabric were tiny bones.

"Keep it at arm's length!" Aunt Thomasin cautioned. "Then pop it in the bucket. Don't forget the charm!" She returned to her own search and, only moments later, found one almost identical to mine.

Walking away from each other, we continued our search.

Placed along the twine, at regular intervals, were more poison tethers. Most of them were of the same design, a woven circle of twigs hung with bones, the only difference being the type of bone attached. Several had birds' feet whilst others had larger leg bones. The more gruesome were decorated with vertebrae from a variety of animals. I found them repugnant. Their dark magick, black, fetid, and glutinous, scratched against my aura as I recited the charm. My skin crawled each time I dropped one into the bucket. The morning wore on as I followed the string and, by the time I met up with Aunt Thomasin, both our buckets were full. I peered into hers.

"So, they're pretty much all the same."

"Yes."

"Mine all have the same fabric. Do yours?"

"A plaid in mauve, black, and pink? Yes."

"It's kind of old-fashioned isn't it," I said. "Quite a heavy weave too. Not like the modern fabric we get now."

"You're right, Livitha. I'm not certain, but it could be from one of Loveday's dresses. It reminds me of one she used to wear. It's such a long time though, I'm struggling to remember when it was."

Not remembering the past was unusual for Aunt Thomasin and I watched her with a sense of creeping dread as she frowned and attempted to recall the memory. Was the poison beginning to work on her too?

"Of course!" she blurted, "Loveday had a travelling dress in this very fabric. Obviously, it is faded now, but it ... surely it's not her dress!" She peered more closely at the fabric. "It does look old, and Loveday wore the dress to death, but it was such a long time ago. She had it made during Queen Victoria's reign—there was a lot of interest in Scotland at the time as Victoria was very fond of her home in Balmoral and spent a great deal of time up there, so plaid became immensely popular." She grew quiet. "Where would they have gotten her dress from?" Turning to me, placing the bucket on the ground, and taking a step away as though suddenly repulsed, she said, "Does it mean the poisoner has been inside Haligern?"

"We would have noticed, surely? One of the familiars would have sounded an alert, I'm sure."

"We are dealing with someone ruthless. Someone who knows about deep magick. It's not unthinkable that they cast a spell to gain entry—unnoticed."

"It's possible," I agreed. Deeply unhappy with the thought that we were so vulnerable to intrusion, I searched for other alternatives. I didn't have enough experience or knowledge to comment on the use of spells, but it just didn't seem possible that we had had an intruder. Surely our collective receptors would have picked it up. But then, Loveday had been poisoned for weeks before we realised what was really happening. "Loveday can't have worn this dress for decades. Where was it stored? It could have been in one of the outhouses." The thought of it being stored outside was reassuring. "They would be easier to access without us noticing."

"You're right, Liv, but all the same, this is quite shocking. To have our personal possessions rifled through!"

"I know I don't have much knowledge, but have they used this fabric to make the hex more powerful?"

"You are absolutely right, Livitha. That is exactly what they have done." For several moments we were both silent. "Come. We must tear down that nasty death tree and take the lot back to Haligern and burn it to ashes!"

By the time we arrived back at the cottage the sun was low on the horizon, dull behind a cloud-filled sky. A chill breeze brushed my cheeks, but I was glad of the cold; tramping around the perimeter for hours and then dragging back the posts had made me sweat.

With the buckets and posts dumped on the driveway we made our way to the kitchen, but as the door opened to Aunt Beatrice's concerned face, a car rolled into the driveway and pulled up to the front of the house.

"Cotta!" Aunt Thomasin sighed. "Not now!"

Oblivious to us, Dr. Cotta stepped out of his silver BMW, stretched, then retrieved his bag from the back seat. With his bronzed skin and bright white teeth, undimmed by the fog and several months in England, I began to wonder if the tan was fake. He surveyed the house and front garden, and then noticed the buckets and long branches that had formed the death-bringing tree.

"He's seen them!" I hissed as he took several steps towards the debris. Aunt Thomasin remained silent.

"He can't touch them," I said. "They may be poisonous. We have to warn him."

Aunt Thomasin batted a hand in my direction. "Curiosity killed the cat."

"You can't be serious!"

"Well ..."

Shocked at her callousness, I tried to distract him, but he was intent on the buckets. I had to act. "No!" I shouted, sprinting across the gravel. His hand hovered above the bucket, frozen in surprise in the act of reaching down.

"No! Don't touch it!" I blurted. My intention was to scoop down to grab the bucket but instead, having gained speed like a rhino at full charge, I failed to stop. Still at a run, and bending to retrieve the bucket, I bowled into Dr. Cotta, my head ramming into his hip. He emitted a surprised grunt as he toppled sideways and, unable to maintain his balance, thudded to the gravel. My journey wasn't over, and I tripped on his leg as it kicked up, then fell to a sprawl across his torso. His grunt, this time, was accompanied by pain. Within a second, the chaos of the fall cleared, and I faced him, nose to nose, in a moment of excruciating embarrassment.

The eyes that locked to mine were filled with shock, and then he smiled.

"I am so sorry!" I blurted, horribly aware of my ample bosom resting on his chest. The ground could open up and swallow me down and I wouldn't complain. "Sorry! So sorry!" I blustered, scrabbling at the gravel to gain purchase. I managed to push myself back but hovered over his hips. And then my arms began to give way! This was not happening. My biceps burned with the effort of holding my weight. *No! No! No!* Along with my arms, which were held in a trembling lock, my foot began to slip in the gravel. If either gave way, I was doomed! My reputation shot to pieces and my psyche scorched with the memory of falling face first into his ... zipper! Gathering all my strength, like a jack-in-the-box, I pushed away from his looming groin, achieving a twisting backflip as graceful as a beached porpoise. I landed with a thud beside the bucket, my face inches away from its galvanized side.

Breathless, I lay prone, my cheeks burning with fiery mortification. A cackle then a snort erupted from behind me. I twisted to push myself up, but a large, bronzed hand appeared. I took it but couldn't meet Dr. Cotta's eyes. "Thanks," I mumbled, my cheeks now scorched.

"No worries. I guess you didn't want me to check out what was in the bucket," he said gesturing to the metal pail at my feet.

"Oh, yes. No! I mean ... you mustn't touch them."

"Oh?" Still curious, he peered into the bucket. "Just looks like a bunch of twigs and rags and ... Is that an animal spine?"

"It's a-"

"Vertebrae?" His frown deepened and he reached into the bucket. "And are those ... ravens?"

"Yes," Aunt Euphemia replied over my 'No!' as I reached down and grabbed the bucket, swinging it away from his grasping hand. Obviously, my previous calamitous efforts to stop him had made no dent in his curiosity.

He pulled back his hand as though scorched.

"Sorry!" I blurted again. "But you can't touch it."

He shot me a confused glance that was filled with suspicion. "Why?"

"We've discovered that someone is laying poison in the woods and it is killing the wildlife," Aunt Thomasin answered.

"Oh! I see. Well, that's just awful!"

"It is. We've been collecting the evidence. So ... the poison may do you harm if you touch it." She held up her gloved hands.

"Ah! Yes, I see." He stood back and brushed his hands together, as though displacing invisible particles.

"Sorry," I said, apologizing for my outburst. "I didn't want you to get any of it on your hands." I held up my gloved hand. "See, we're protected."

"Yep, I can see that. So, who do you think it is that's trying to poison the animals?"

Again, I was stumped and again Aunt Thomasin came to my rescue. "Well, they're poisoning the rabbits, so we don't think they're poachers, at least not for meat, but they may be collecting them for their skins."

"Rabbit-skin coats are quite fashionable this year," Aunt Beatrice colluded.

"They are?" Dr. Cotta's frown returned.

"So I've heard."

"And the ravens?"

"Feathers!" I blurted. "And ... and their skulls. People collect them and I've even seen them decorated and mounted in a frame."

Dr. Cotta bit his lower lip down onto his teeth and nodded. "Okay, sounds plausible, I guess."

There was no way he believed my bizarre explanation, but I sensed he didn't want to seem rude by disagreeing.

"So, Dr. Cotta," said Aunt Thomasin, completely unflustered, "How can we help you?"

"I've actually come to check on Mr. Wolfreston," He held up his medical bag.

"Did Loveday call you?" I asked, my discomfort suddenly evaporating into concern. "Is he worse?"

Dr. Cotta raised his hand as though in surrender. "It's just a courtesy call. Mrs. Wolfreston didn't call me but has his health declined?"

"He's not well," I admitted.

"Then it's a good job I came by." He offered me a kindly smile. I forced one back, the sensation of dread returning. A doctor checking on Uncle Raif's declining health made it all the more real.

Aunt Thomasin stepped between us. "If you'll follow me, Dr. Cotta, I shall ask Raif if he consents to seeing you."

"Absolutely. Consent. If you lead the way, I'm happy to follow." His broad smile wasn't returned but he followed Aunt Thomasin up the steps. The front door creaked as Aunt Thomasin pushed against it to get it fully open. My heart sank. The door no longer fit properly in its frame, a sign of the spreading decay.

Chapter Nine

The stairs creaked as Dr. Cotta descended, his steps becoming slower the further down he came. When he appeared at the kitchen doorway the bright smile he arrived with, had gone.

"Come in doctor," Aunt Beatrice said with forced pleasantry. "Would you like a cup of tea?"

He managed a smile but declined. "No, thank you, but we do need to have a talk about Mr. Wolfreston. He's really not very well. He appears to be suffering from delusions."

"Delusions, Dr. Cotta?"

"Yes. He seems to think he's living during a past time."

We remained silent. Uncle Raif had increasingly been regressing to memories of his past life, particularly his youth during the late sixteenth century.

"He thinks he's a Tudor gentleman and keeps talking about a place called Kedleston." Dr. Cotta managed a wan smile but remained serious. "I think he would benefit from an assessment, but Mrs. Wolfreton is refusing to give permission for him to be admitted to hospital-"

"Well! That's just not necessary," blurted Aunt Thomasin. "Raif was always interested in history."

Dr. Cotta looked taken aback by her outburst. "I can understand that. I love history too," he offered in placatory tones, "but Mr. Wolfreston appears to be very weak."

"We're taking good care of him, Dr. Cotta," Aunt Euphemia added. "He's getting three meals a day, plus elevenses and supper. He's getting plenty to drink."

"Well, if you're sure. I'd feel happier if he were admitted for observations, but if you say he is eating and drinking ... but listen, if he deteriorates further there is help available. Sometimes personalities change ... if you need help, just let me know."

Defensive energy crackled through my aunts but Dr. Cotta's desire to help us seemed genuine. "Thank you," I offered as my aunts maintained a stony silence. "We appreciate your concern."

"It's my job, Liv."

"I know, but coming out here ... I'm not aware of any other doctors that make house calls these days. It's good of you to care."

He nodded and then caught sight of the damaged chimney breast. "What happened?" He took a step towards the cracked mantle and pile of bricks in the hearth.

"Oh, it just needs a bit of maintenance."

He cast me a concerned glance. "I'd say more than a bit." Stepping up to the hearth he ran a hand over the crack. Shards of lime mortar sprinkled onto his shoe. "I think you should have a structural survey done, Liv. I noticed the front door was heavy too. It could be subsidence."

I ran with his idea. "Yes! That's exactly what it is."

Scanning the ceiling he noticed the other cracks. "There too! And when I came down the stairs they creaked. I hadn't noticed that before."

"Oh, they've always creaked," I lied. "It's such an old house. It was built hundreds of years ago."

"But you'll get a surveyor in?"

I nodded. "I'm talking to Mike, our builder, tomorrow." Another lie. "He's used to renovating properties and I'm hoping he'll give us some advice."

Placated, but with another glance at the broken chimney breast, Dr. Cotta said his goodbyes to my aunts and then I walked him to the door. It was an effort to pull it open.

"I can take a look at it for you," he offered.

I shook my head. "That's kind, but as I said, Mike's coming over tomorrow. It's all in hand."

"Right'o. Bonza."

At his car he hovered, obviously wanting to say something. Was he going to insist that Uncle Raif be admitted to hospital? Was he going to mention me nearly falling headfirst into his privates! "Liv, I've been invited to a wedding," he said. He seemed reticent. "I was wondering if you'd like to be my plus one?"

I let out a sigh of relief that nearly erupted as hysteria in one of those moments of extreme discomfort. He threw me a confused glance.

"I'm sorry!" I managed, relieved that I had an honest excuse to turn him down for a change. "I'm already going with my aunts. But if you're going too ... then I'll see you there?" I offered.

With a disappointed smile he gave an understanding nod. "Bonza, Liv."

For a moment I thought he was going to kiss me goodbye, but he simply smiled as he slipped behind the wheel of his car then drove away. Relieved, I watched him go then turned my attention to the buckets filled with dead ravens and poison tethers, and the demolished death tree by their side. All sat at the edge of the drive waiting to be burned. We had work to do.

Bonfires were lit and, with the poisonous debris hissing and crackling as it burned, it was decided that we would create our own ring of magic, but this one was to be for protection and not for harm. Twigs were collected from the trees closest to the house along with lengths of ivy. Under instruction from Aunt Euphemia who had found a suitable charm in her grimoire, we wove the twigs and ivy into circles. Protective runes were fashioned from twigs and secured in the centre of each circle with twine made from hemp that Loveday had spun several years ago. Each protective tether was dipped into a glittering bath of mugwort and sage infused with sprinkles of our magick. As each woven circle of power was dipped, we chanted together then took them out to sit beneath the moon's rays as Euphemia invoked the power of the moon.

"Invoking the moon is powerful, Livitha," she said as we broke our own circle. "I would like to gift this charm to you, for your own grimoire."

"So kind!" Aunt Beatrice clapped her hands.

"Selfless," Aunt Thomasin said.

"Thank you," I added not quite sure why it was a selfless act.

"It's because once you have taken the charm, claiming it as your own by writing it into your own grimoire, it holds less power for Euphemia," Aunt Beatrice explained.

I realised the import of the gift. "But Aunt Euphemia, I don't want to take it if it means it won't work for you."

"You must," she replied. "I insist. I haven't used it for more than five hundred years, and I have others that could take its place. I think it fitting that you should take it."

My other aunts nodded in enthusiastic agreement.

"Sisters, now that we have created the circle, I think it may be the time for our gift-giving to take place."

"But what of Loveday?"

"Ah, yes."

"Let's wait until tomorrow. If this charm works-"

"Which it will!"

"Yes, of course Euphemia, it is just a figure of speech! After it has begun to work ... Then we will gather to give Livitha our gifts.

"Agreed."

"Splendid!"

"Okay," I agreed, a little bemused.

"Now, time to go in. It is cold out here."

"It's quite late."

"Past Livitha's bedtime!"

I sighed but couldn't help a chuckle. Despite the fact that I was fifty years old, my aunts would always mother me. It wasn't something I was unhappy about. "It really isn't that late," I said with a smile.

"Well, then it's time for cocoa," beamed Aunt Beatrice.

With hot cocoa steaming in large mugs, we gathered at the kitchen table and were quickly drawn back to leafing through the grimoires. Soon, leafing turned into studious efforts to look for more powerful spells of protection, and hexes against our enemy.

But whilst the aunts pored over their books for charms, spells, and hexes that could do the job, I searched through Arthur for any hint of a clue as to who the perpetrator could be. Without the fire to warm us, witch lights infused with a heat-radiating energy hovered close to the hearth. But as the evening drew on, their output waned along with my aunts' energy. Worse, as midnight approached, I was no closer to discovering a reasonable lead.

Tired, I leaned back in my chair, stretching my arms out to relieve the stiffness across my shoulders.

"Perhaps we should go to bed," Aunt Thomasin suggested. "We're all beginning to suffer from tiredness.

"Just a little longer," I said. "I'm sure there must be clues amongst the stories Loveday has written in Arthur." I had been working through the text but was still no further than a quarter of the way through.

"You may be correct, Livitha, but Arthur is a vast tome."

"It's certainly taking some time to get through!" I agreed.

"That's because what is evident is not what is."

I pulled a frown. "I'm not sure what you mean."

Despite her tiredness, Aunt Euphemia chuckled. "Well, Arthur does look very chunky, but haven't you noticed that no matter how many pages you read, your progress seems horribly slow?"

I sighed. "I have!"

"That's because there are hidden pages, invisible to the eye when you view the book, but as you read, the text appears, so, you may read ten pages, but another ten take its place, unseen until you give them your attention."

"I see. I guess ..."

"Loveday has been filling that book in for centuries, Livitha. It would be as big as the *Complete English Oxford Dictionary* if it were to appear in its true physical form."

"Wow!" I said. "That would be huge."

"She's kept it as a sort of diary too, as have we all."

"Then there must be something inside. Something that will lead us to the poisoner. It has to be an enemy and somewhere in these pages there will be a reference to someone she has crossed or ticked off!"

"There will be many," Aunt Beatrice chuckled. "Loveday never was one to mince her words."

"But it also has to be someone close by. If they have one of Loveday's old dresses, then they've been here."

"Or at least visited. Remember, she can fly or uses intra-dimensional travel."

"True, Thomasin," agreed Aunt Beatrice. "And the plaid fabric did look similar to her old travelling dress. She did love it although I thought it a little garish myself."

"There's no knowing how long this enemy has had the dress."

"I'll have to talk to Aunt Loveday about it," I explained. "I have to know where she had it stored."

"That will have to wait."

"Yes, until tomorrow."

"She should be feeling a little better tomorrow, once the charm starts its work."

"It will at least dilute the poison."

"Indeed it will."

Eyes burning with tiredness, I considered Arthur, his pages open before me, every inch of each carefully prepared skin filled with text and symbols. I took the last sip of cocoa from my cup. It was cold, but I was past caring. "If I just focus on the accounts of her life, then I can get through him quicker," I suggested.

"Your dedication is touching, Livitha, but I fear by the time you discover anything it will be too late."

"Perhaps Arthur should be the one who tells us what is useful among his pages?"

"Ah, that is a wonderful idea, Livitha, but only Loveday can help him reveal that."

I sighed with resignation and made an annoyed scribble on the page of my notebook. I had written several notes, but nothing that was of real use and, with eyes burning, admitted defeat and went to bed.

Chapter Ten

The following morning, proof that our circle of protective charms was working, came in the form of Aunt Loveday in the kitchen. Miraculously, she even had colour in her cheeks. She still appeared frail, but the gleam had reappeared in her eyes where only rheumy dullness had lain like an opaque film the day before.

I greeted her with a huge, relieved, smile.

"Good morning, Livitha," she said from her place at the table and sipped her tea with a hand that didn't tremble.

It was a miracle! "It *is* a good morning!" I replied with joy. "A fantastic morning." I half expected bluetits and mice to sing a chorus!

"Someone got out on the right side of bed!" Aunt Beatrice chuckled.

"Well, yes!" I replied with a smile I couldn't hide as I glanced at Aunt Loveday. "I just know that everything is going to be alright."

"Who stole Livitha and replaced her with Pollyanna?" my aunt joked.

For the next half an hour we chatted and laughed, ignoring the terrible hex that had been devastating our lives. I drank two cups of coffee and ate one of Aunt Beatrice's bread rolls spread with butter and marmalade. If the broken mantle and unlit fire hadn't been there to remind me of our predicament, it would have been a perfect morning and I felt much happier about having to leave the cottage to go to work; with the shop newly opened, we had that pressure to contend with too. Talk turned to our work of scouring the grimoires the previous evening. I was keen to continue reading through Arthur but with Aunt Loveday's energy revived, if only a fraction, she had asked for the book.

As Aunt Beatrice busied herself about the kitchen and my other aunts sat with their grimoires open, I felt at a loss. I waited several minutes, writing notes in my notebook whilst wracking my brain for some question to ask Aunt Loveday that may give us a lead on who was attacking her when Aunt Thomasin broke the silence. "I know that this may not be the best of times, but I think it is time that Livitha had her own grimoire."

The other aunts stopped reading and gave her their attention.

"Why, yes! I think so too."

Aunt Loveday lifted Arthur's pages and pulled out an unused booklet. "I was going to wait until *The Gathering* at Winter Solstice to give this to you, but, given the circumstances ... Here, this is for you." The hand-sewn booklet of prepared skins was nearly A4 size; my grimoire would be as large as Arthur!

"It's beautiful!" I said admiring the silky-smooth finish of the pages.

"It is a quire of vellum—calf's skin. It will last a witch's lifetime," she smiled. "Paper just will not do for a grimoire. It must be vellum or some other animal skin—paper will just not stand the test of time."

"I have a gift too!" Aunt Euphemia held out a narrow box. It opened to reveal a glossy black fountain pen with a gold nib.

"It's beautiful," I said. "Thank you!"

"Me too. I have a gift too!" From behind her back, Aunt Beatrice brought out a small, corked flagon.

"Cider?" I asked, making a weak joke.

"No, silly! It's ink. Raven black and based on a recipe used by Eadfrith who wrote the Lindisfarne Gospels, although I think mine is an improvement. His book is still beautiful today and he wrote it hundreds of years ago."

"The earliest years of the eighth century, Beatrice," Aunt Loveday added. "He was a good, if misguided man, but such ... now what is that modern word? Ah, yes. He was a terrible workaholic. The book took him more than ten years to create, but it was so very beautiful!"

Aunt Loveday's eyes glazed as she regressed to her memories and Aunt Thomasin held out her gift.

"But you've already given me a gift. The charm."

"We will all gift you a charm or spell-"

"Or hex."

"Yes, or hex. Thank you, Beatrice."

She held out a roll of soft leather and bundle of leather thongs. "It is to make the cover."

"So, I'm to make the book myself?"

"Yes, of course."

"It is the only way."

"It makes it personal. The book becomes bound to you."

"So," said Aunt Loveday, "now you have your very own grimoire starter kit. I do wish we had been able to give it to you at a better time, but ... Oh, I'm not sure ... If I don't recover ..." Tears glistened in her eyes. "Oh, I just cannot lose Raif!"

"You won't!" I blurted. "We're going to find out who's doing this and stop them!"

As my aunts comforted Loveday the front door creaked open, and Mrs. Driscoll arrived for her morning cleaning session. Aunt Thomasin cast a quick charm to make Mrs. Driscoll oblivious to the grimoires just as she stepped into the kitchen.

"Good morning, ladies. Oh," she said noticing Loveday. "It is good to see you up and about, Loveday. You must be feeling better."

"I am, thank you Celeste."

"I was just thinking about you on my way up here and hoping it would be so. Must have been a terrible bug to make you so ill. Seems you're not the only one as has caught it though." She hung her coat up and retrieved her full apron from her bag, slipping her arms through the sleeves and forming the ties into a bow with deft fingers.

"Is there a bug going round the village?"

"Well, there's always something, but no, I was referring to Aggie Sampson. She's aged terribly these past weeks. Must be a terrible bug to bring someone so low. Thankfully, she has good neighbours and Mrs. Berrywell is helping out. Poor woman can't even get to the shops now."

"Poor lady," I commiserated. "Perhaps it is flu? That can knock people out, especially the elderly."

"True," she replied, "though it's the way she's aged that really struck me. One week she was the picture of health, and the next she's haggard, stooped, and fragile. If I didn't know better, I'd say she was knocking on a hundred years old, and not a healthy one either, but I know she can't be more than sixty. Bless her!"

My aunts shared questioning glances whilst agreeing that it was a terrible shame and that they hoped she would soon get better.

"Well, I'll start in the drawing room seeing as you're all busy in here." As she turned to leave, the broken mantlepiece caught her attention. "Oh dear! It is worse than the other day."

"It's all in hand. We've decided to have a structural survey done," I lied. "They'll be here next week."

Satisfied, she stepped into the hall. A tile chinked, and I noticed with dread that the floor was now uneven.

"I'll be there in a few minutes," Aunt Euphemia called as Mrs. Driscoll pushed the drawing room door open. It too had become stiff as though swelled with damp.

Once out of earshot my aunts began to talk.

"She's talking about Aggie Sampson!"

"She was here for your initiation, Livitha."

"She looked the picture of health then."

"Well, she's certainly not now!"

"Do you think someone could be poisoning her too?"

"It's possible."

"If it is true," I said, "then we can start to narrow down the suspects."

"How so?"

"Well, if she is being poisoned, there must be some connection."

"I see. Well then you must visit her. Take some of Euphemia's elixir and see if what Mrs. Driscoll says is true."

"I can go after I close the shop. How will I know if it is true?"

"You will sense it."

"And smell it!"

"Smell it?"

"Yes, smell it. Have you not noticed that pungent aroma? It is faint, but it is the same as the tethers we collected from the buckets."

I sniffed. There *was* a faint but unpleasant smell in the air.

"Brimstone!"

"It is the stench of dark magick from the other realm."

"When you visit, do be careful. The old crone can be tricky."

"How so?"

"She came into her powers at the height of the Cromwellian uprising. Despite her witchiness, she has a puritanical streak."

"Oh? Is she religious?"

"Oh, no! Not puritanical in that way. She just will not tolerate some ideas. She's a fusty old stick."

"Oh. Right."

"Yes. She's very lucky that she doesn't share that stye with Old Mawde." Aunt Beatrice cackled. "The way she and Loveday used to fight!" She chuckled, shaking her head as she wiped wet hands on her pinny.

"Her being ill does rule her out as a suspect," Aunt Thomasin added. "I had her on my list of possible enemies."

"Fiddlesticks, Thomasin. Aggie Sampson may be cantankerous, but she's not murderous."

"I trust no one."

With that declaration, my Aunts returned to their chores and I readied myself to go into work with the promise of visiting Aggie Sampson after closing the shop.

Chapter Eleven

After the grand opening fiasco, and the forced closure as Vlad and I worked to discover who had killed his girlfriend Mindy, things had settled into a better routine and I had managed to open regularly and on time, despite the problems at the cottage. Today I was running late, and I was mortified to see several shoppers outside the locked shop as I approached. Before I had a chance to park, they trundled away, obviously disgruntled. I parked hurriedly and flung open the car door, only just stopping myself from calling after them. Opening late was unprofessional but calling after potential customers to shout 'Yoohoo! I'm here. Don't go! Come back!' would make us look desperate. Unlocking the shop door, I flipped the sign to 'Open' and paused to savour the smell and absorb the energy. Softly aromatic, the smell was of lavender, calendula, and sweet honey mixed with sage and mugwort. Taking a deep breath, I let the shop's calming energy smooth over me then closed the door, realising that I was smiling for the first time in days. Uncle Raif's ill-health, the deterioration of the cottage, and now Aunt Loveday's very obvious and rapid decline into frail old age, had taken their toll and my own energy had been low. Getting away from the cottage, with its fractious energy, was liberating, plus I was itching to visit Aggie Sampson and see if our suspicions that she too was being poisoned were true.

I busied myself dusting and filling the shelves and making note of which products we needed to restock. There were a number of lotions that were becoming our bestsellers and last week several customers had travelled quite some distance to purchase them. We hadn't done any advertising and even the hoped for write up in the local newspaper hadn't appeared. However, for this, I was thankful. A piece detailing the disastrous appearance of Vlad's Whitby wives and their vampiric miniature Pomeranian, would have brought us notoriety. As it was, rumour had encouraged vampire-loving fans into action and produced a flow of Goths to the shop. Their interest had quickly waned however, and they had instinctively gravitated towards Martha's shop where her arcane curios and charismatic nature suited their aesthetic far better.

The day passed slowly. We'd had a variety of customers including one who had travelled fifty miles for a pot of our anti-ageing cream that her aunt, who lived in the village, swore by. The customer had been amazed at the change in her aunt's complexion since she started using the cream. Another woman came in asking for something to protect her house as she had started to feel unwelcome there. She had also asked for an appointment with Loveday. Despite Loveday's current state, I'd booked an appointment several weeks in the future, sure that by then our problems would have been resolved. When a man came in, complete with mud-stained wellingtons and flat cap asking for Loveday to come by and bless his allotment, I realised just how important she was to the wider community too. I promised to speak to her and pencilled in a date for the blessing.

With my shop chores done, and during a lull between customers, my mind turned to Lady Heskitt's forthcoming wedding, and Garrett. Would he be at there? With everything that was going on, the wedding had been pushed to the back of my mind and I had made no effort to sort out an outfit and hadn't booked any appointments to have my hair or nails done. Not that I'd ever been big on self-maintenance, but it was a high society wedding and the least I could do was turn up looking relatively polished. Despite a niggling anxiety about going, I had no intention of visiting the hairdressers or beauty salon. I would just have to make more than my usual self-grooming effort. However, at this late stage, the best I was going to be able to achieve was a quick shaving of my legs with an old razor, a blow dry of my hair, and a check for any wayward facial growth. I did have a set of curling tongs that Pascal had bought me last Christmas, but I was no kind of pro in the hair curling department. Of course, I could have a go at my eyebrows too. But what on earth was I going to wear? Would anything remotely decent that I owned still fit me? I was going to look like a super-frump! I let out a groan, confident that no one would hear. Garrett, in comparison, I was sure, would look suave and handsome.

My stomach rolled and I was filled with yearning sadness. He still hadn't called to ask me out.

Ask him out yourself!

I had played with the idea of being a little more forthright. *Why not ask him out?* I was a modern woman, after all! The thought made me squirm. What if he said no! What if he thought less of me for asking? I battled with my thoughts.

I should wait for him to ask me.

That could be forever, most likely never,
So, ask him!
But that could make me look desperate or even a man eater!

I wasn't sure the situation put me in the cougar category, but the thought made me feel a little grubby, nevertheless.

We make our own luck in this world.

Yes, but it will be your bad luck if he thinks you're being too forward.

Being too forward! Surely women have moved beyond that.

Well, then, if you're so progressive, why don't you join an online dating agency?

I'd rather be swallowed into the pit of hell!

At this point I refused to discuss the situation with myself anymore. I'd rather die an old maid than join an online dating agency, plus it wouldn't help me get Garrett's attention.

Unless he was on there too?
He'd never be on there!
Why don't you take a look?
No! Absolutely not!

With my thoughts filled with impending social doom, and mulling over excuses as to why I shouldn't attend the wedding, the bell above the door tinkled and Dr. Cotta walked in. Handsome as always, the blue of his eyes was bright against his bronzed skin and I couldn't help looking for tell-tale tan lines or evidence of paler skin around the eyes. A few more months in England and he would be as pasty as the rest of us and then I'd know for sure whether his colour was the result of the Australian sun's rays or came from a bottle or sunbed. His smile was broad and friendly. Inwardly, I cringed; I was being ungenerous—he had only ever been kind to me.

"Afternoon, Liv," he said with a flash of brilliant, perfectly aligned, white teeth.

"Afternoon," I replied with my best 'I'm so pleased to see you' smile, determined to lift myself from the swamp of negative emotions.

Stepping into the shop, he glanced around. "It's the first time I've been here since the opening," he said. "I didn't get a chance to look round properly—there was so much going on!"

I laughed. "It was certainly an interesting evening."

He walked across to the shelves where the cleansing sticks were displayed. "I thought your drama with the vampire brides was genius!" There was no hint of sarcasm. "Great way of getting noticed."

"Well ... it's a tough world in the apothecary business," I joked.

"It is. Now," he said, "do you have anything for a bit of a sprained ankle. I pulled it this morning when I went out for a run."

My surprise must have been obvious because he laughed and said, "Yes, doctors like natural remedies too."

"Of course! Well, yes! We've got a lovely lotion that my Aunt Thomasin makes, it's a recipe she's had for centuries-" I clamped my lips together, alarmed that I had nearly begun to explain that Aunt Thomasin had had the recipe in her grimoire for at least three centuries and had recently perfected it. Gathering my senses, I said, "Rosemary. It contains rosemary which has been used for centuries to help with inflammation."

"It has," he agreed. "And there are plenty of scientific studies to show that it works. I'll take some."

I found a small jar and rang it through the till. As he turned to leave, he paused, and the true reason for his visit became clear.

"Liv ... I'm concerned about your aunt and uncle. They seem very frail. I really think that they need to be seen ... by professionals. Perhaps a stay in hospital would be beneficial? I'd like to-"

"They're both fine!" I blurted. "Aunt Loveday was downstairs this morning. She's feeling so much better."

"Ah ... good. And Mr. Wolfreston?"

"He's fine too."

"I have a duty of care, Liv ..."

"But they're fine!" My heart raced. "They'll be fine!"

"Well ... I'll check back in next week, Liv. The elderly can take a turn for the worse within hours. If you have any concerns, any at all ... you must call me."

I nodded though I couldn't manage a smile. My defences were definitely up.

"I'm here to help, Liv."

"I know, and I appreciate it, but they're fine."

He nodded, smiled, then left the shop. I ran to the door and locked it with shaking hands and turned the sign to 'Closed'. What did he mean 'duty of care'? That he'd have them admitted to hospital? Removing them from Haligern, the only place where they had any protection, would be fatal. I had to do something to stop the poison that was causing their deterioration, and quick. With renewed determination, I decided to visit Aggie Sampson. The shop would have to remain closed.

As I stood with my back to the door, heart pounding, someone knocked. Startled, I turned to see Lina. Relieved to see a friendly face, I opened the door.

"Closing early?"

"Oh …" I checked my watch. "Yeah, just a few minutes, I guess. I'm going to a wedding tomorrow and need to figure out what to wear," I waffled. The excuse was the best I could come up with.

"You okay?" she asked. "You look a little flustered."

I wafted a hand at my cheeks. "Just a hot flush. Menopause!" I raised my brow in a martyred grimace. She remained in the doorway and, too polite to ask her to leave, I stepped aside.

"Are you sure? It is nearly closing time after all."

"No, it's okay. I can stay open for a little longer."

"If you're sure you're sure?"

I resisted looking at my watch. "Yes, I'm sure."

She offered me a friendly, thankful smile. "Oh, that's great. It's just I've heard such good things about one of your creams and I've run out of my usual one, so I thought … Do you mind if I look around?"

"Yes, of course. I mean no!" I managed a laugh. "Please … look around and take your time. There's no hurry." This was a lie. I was more than keen to see Aggie Sampson. "So, what was the cream you were looking for?"

"Celeste said it's one you make. I think it's called 'Euphemia's Youth Dew.'"

"Oh, yes. I know exactly which one she means. It's our best seller. Actually, today I had a customer travel over fifty miles to purchase a jar."

"It must really work!"

"Well, she does have relatives in the village, so I guess she was killing two birds with one stone ..."

"Still, she came in to buy it. It must be magic!"

She threw me a glance that I ignored and instead brushed off her comment. "Well, she did say it worked like magic for her aunt."

"I have to admit, your aunts do look amazing. And Celeste's skin glows too. And your skin is lovely. So smooth and clear. Do you use it yourself?"

We continued to talk and once again fell into comfortable conversation. She was so interesting and easy to talk to. I found myself wanting to share all of my troubles with her although managed to resist. After half an hour of chatting and laughing, I felt invigorated and when she suggested we meet up for a coffee one day soon, I eagerly agreed. It would be so good to have a friend in the village, someone who understood me and really knew how to carry a conversation.

Chapter Twelve

Aggie Sampson's home was only a short distance from the shop, and I arrived within ten minutes of locking up. After leaving the main hub of the village, which consisted of a small but well-known convenience store that doubled as the post office, the old newsagent's shop which was now Martha's *Arcane Treasures, Haligern Cottage Apothecary,* two pubs, a clock repair shop, a pharmacist, a Chinese takeaway, and a fish and chip shop, I walked up the road towards the house.

Lined with a variety of houses, the street was quaint. None of the houses dated much after 1900 and many were Georgian, and carefully maintained whilst retaining their original period details. An abandoned Methodist Chapel had been converted to flats and the only nod to modern life were the cars parked along the street, the streetlights, and the telephone wires that stretched overhead. The village was far older than this street would suggest, however.

At the top of the road the space widened to a grassy hillock upon the top of which sat a church built before the eleventh century. Like so many churches, it had been built directly on top of a pagan site of worship. Directly opposite was Aggie Sampson's cottage, like the church, it dated from the medieval period and sat on land that had been inhabited from the first century. People had populated the surrounding area for millennia and a Roman mosaic floor had been uncovered in a local field to the west of the village. Although many of the houses along the road were elegant, with bay windows fronted by gardens of clipped privet and symmetrical topiary, Aggie's cottage, with its quirky, asymmetrical charm and abundance of climbing roses, was my favourite.

Smoke trailed from a barley twist chimney as I swung open the iron gate. A short path led to the front door where a single, but large bow window, sat to the side allowing a glimpse into the living room where a fire burned low in the hearth. Aggie sat beside the fire, gnarled hands resting on the arms of her high-backed chair. Obviously asleep, her chin rested on her chest and a crocheted blanket lay across her knees. Hair, still thick, lay as a long, white plait over her shoulder. I remembered her from my initiation ceremony. There she had been as elegant and sprightly as my aunts although at least a decade younger. Now she looked to be at the frail end of elderly.

Mrs. Driscoll had mentioned a neighbour and I presumed it must be her who had placed the blanket over Aggie's knee and the tea tray on the table by her side. The cup of tea remained full and the plate of biscuits beside it untouched.

Stepping away from the window, I knocked on the door repeatedly to get her attention, and minutes passed before the curtains twitched and I caught sight of her wrinkled face peering at me through the window. I waved and she disappeared but when she finally came to the door, she didn't open it.

"Who is it?" Her voice, thin and reedy, was unsteady with age.

"It's Livitha Erikson," I called back. "I've brought you a tonic from my aunts."

The door opened a fraction.

Although I had seen her dozing in the chair and peeping from the curtain, I was unprepared at the drastic difference in her appearance since our last meeting.

"I ..."

Her eyes flickered with pain as she noticed my reaction and I felt that pain as a wave of angst-filled energy.

She opened the door a little further and shuffled backwards. "Come in, dear."

The fire made the room warm and stuffy, but she shivered as though chilled and then lowered herself back into her seat.

I sat on the sofa opposite and pulled the tonic out of my bag. "Aunt Euphemia sent this tonic. It's one of her fortifying elixirs. She told me to tell you that she has added a little extra, just for you."

"Ah, Euphemia. We always were good friends. I haven't seen her for some time though. Not for many years."

Aggie Sampson, just like Aunt Loveday, was struggling with her memory; the last time she had spoken to Aunt Euphemia had been at my Initiation ceremony where they had shared a jug of a pink and fizzing cocktail.

"Would you like me to pour some of the tonic into your tea?"

She agreed and I put five drops of elixir into the cup then held it out for her to drink from. Within minutes, she seemed a little more animated.

"Aggie, you seem tired," I ventured. "I don't want to upset you, but you seem to have aged since I last saw you."

"Nothing I do is working!" she blurted. "Every time I try to use my magick it just drains me, and I age quicker."

"The same has happened to Loveday."

"Hah!" she said with a glitter in her eyes. "Couldn't happen to a more deserving crone!"

I was surprised. "I'm not sure what the history is between you two, but I think that you're both being poisoned by the same witch. We've found evidence of black magick at Haligern."

Piercing green eyes focused on me. "Tell me."

I explained about the death tree. She nodded, energized. "That's it! That's exactly it."

"Do you have any idea who would be doing this? Someone who holds a grudge against both you and Aunt Loveday?"

"Hah! There are so many ... but no one in particular comes to mind."

"Do you think that you could give it some thought. Loveday is so sick, and Raif too."

"Oh! Raif too! That is terrible news. Of course, I will do my best. Euphemia's tonic has taken the edge off the muddle that was in my mind."

"She said she'll pop round later. She has some charms that may help."

"I'd appreciate that. My magick seems so weak now."

Before leaving, I made a fresh pot of tea. As I placed it on her table, she asked me to wait and instructed me to fetch her grimoire from a bureau sat at the side of the chimney breast. Smaller than Arthur, it was made in similar style and was filled to bursting with quires of parchment. Tooled onto its leather cover were pagan symbols and runes. Holding it on her lap, she leafed through the pages.

"You're to be presented at the *Gathering* this solstice," she stated.

"Yes."

"Pass me a pen. I need paper too." She gestured to the bureau. I took a pen from a stone pot and a spiralbound notebook and passed them to her. She copied out a charm then ripped the page from the notebook. "Take this," she said thrusting the page at me. "I may not be here when the time comes. This is my gift."

I took the paper. The charm was written in runes that I couldn't decipher.

"You like it?" she asked with a wry smile.

I had to be honest. "I can't read it."

She huffed. "A mis-spent youth! What are they teaching them these days! You have a grimoire, don't you? A book?"

"No, not yet. At least, I haven't made it yet."

Again, she huffed and then, with surprising agility, stood and walked from the room. Impressed at the power of Aunt Euphemia's elixir, I waited for her to return, listening as she padded across the floor above me then came back down the stairs. She stopped at the living room doorway and leant against it, the effort of going upstairs having taken its toll. Taking her elbow, I guided her back to the highchair and then dripped more elixir into her empty cup before filling it with tea as she regained her breath.

"Give me a moment."

"I'm not in a hurry."

Embers glowed in the hearth and I threw in another log to feed the dying fire. She stared at the flames as though in a trance.

Minutes passed as she gazed at the crackling log before she came back to the present. "Ah! The ancestors' call is loud today. I must be nearing my end."

"I'm not going to let that happen. That's why I'm here—to try and find out who's doing this and stop them."

A wan smile rose to her lips. "I wish you well in your quest, Livitha, daughter of Soren, but I fear it may be too late. I can feel my faculties slipping with each passing hour. Now, we can talk about this in a minute. Here!" She held out a roll of creamy vellum. "I have been saving this for you. A quire for your own book. I'm sure Loveday and the coven have begun to school you in our magick but taking knowledge from us all will increase your power. This quire – she coughed and caught her breath – is made from a roe deer's hide hunted under the Wolf Moon of 1970."

"My birth year!"

"Yes. We have waited such a long time for you."

"And you prepared this yourself?"

"I did."

I unrolled the vellum to reveal a booklet of expertly prepared skins, each almost as thin as paper. "They're beautiful."

"Thank you. And whatever you write upon them will be forever hidden from those who do not have permission to read them."

I remembered the blank pages in Aunt Loveday's own grimoire. I hadn't realised they were filled with secrets.

After promising to visit again soon, I returned to Haligern and my aunts, frustrated to report that, although I was no closer to discovering the culprit, I was now convinced that Aunt Loveday and Aggie Sampson were being poisoned by the same witch. All I had to do now, was discover who hated them both enough to attempt a double murder!

Chapter Thirteen

The following morning, still damp from my shower, wet hair twisted into a turban, I was sorting through my wardrobe for a wedding outfit when a loud yowl was followed by scratching at my door. Before I had a chance to react, the handle lowered, and the door sprung open. Lucifer pushed through the gap.

"Outside!" he yelled. "On the doorstep. Come!"

"What? I'm not dressed Lucifer!" Used to his demands, and deep in my own anxiety about what exactly I would wear, I turned back to the wardrobe.

Lucifer hissed.

Surprised at his aggression, I turned back to him. "Whatever is it?"

"Come!" he demanded. "Now!"

I noticed then that he was wide-eyed and breathless. Something terrible had happened.

"Give me a minute to get dressed."

He padded about the room with impatience, refusing to explain what the problem was as I hurriedly pulled on underwear, jeans, and a top. Dressed, I followed him down the stairs to the front door.

"Stop!" he commanded as we reached the door. "Beyond this door is something more terrible than ..." He gulped, overcome with emotion. "So, so terrible!"

"Let me past, Lou."

He sniffed.

I placed my hand on the doorknob but overcome with trepidation, I turned to Lucifer. "Tell me what it is, Lucifer."

"It's ..." He faltered, overcome with emotion. "Him!"

I took a breath to steel myself and, with heart hammering, I opened the door.

"He's on the doorstep!" Lucifer rasped as the door swung inwards.

I gasped and sank to my knees.

On the doorstep was a large black raven, its neck obviously broken. "Benny!" I said in horror. For several moments, all I could do was squat on my haunches until the pain in my knees became unbearable. "He's dead!" I whispered. Now shaking, I scooped Lucifer into my arms and hugged him to my chest. He made no effort to pull away and pressed his face into my armpit. Muffled, indecipherable, words followed. The bird lay on the top step, wings neatly folded at its side, clawed feet locked into a curl. Its head hung over the edge of the step. "But he can't be dead! Not Benny."

More muffled words followed then Lucifer pulled his nose out of my armpit. A low and piteous mewl followed. "Oh Benny! Why did it have to be you!" he wailed.

"How did it happen, Lou?"

He shook his head. "I don't know. I've only just returned. I was going to come in through the back door, but something urged me onwards to the front, and then I saw him."

"Was he dead when you found him?"

"He was. I tried to revive him, but it was too late."

"Do you think that he could have flown into the door and hurt himself that way?"

"Only if he was blind! Birds can be stupid, and Benny has flown into windows before, but the door is solid, and black, and obviously not a thoroughfare into the house when it is closed. Even Benny wouldn't be that stupid!"

"Then ..." A glint caught my eye and I crouched to the body. "This is murder!" Thin wire protruded from beneath the bird's head. I pinched one end between my fingers. The body moved. "He was garrotted! Look! This wire is wound around his neck."

"Murder! Why would anyone murder Benny?"

A chill ran through my body. "The same person who is trying to poison Aunt Loveday and Aggie Sampson."

I closed the door. "Lucifer, I'm going to find a box and a cloth to wrap him in."

He nodded and jumped down from my arms then ran back along the hallway to the kitchen. I made my way to one of the outbuildings where we kept the stock of boxes for the apothecary shop. After several minutes I found one and returned to the front step. However, I stalled when it came to picking up Benny's body. I needed gloves. As I crouched beside him my thoughts turned to Aunt Thomasin. She would be devastated!

"Who would be devastated?"

Startled I turned to Aunt Beatrice who had appeared at my side. "You really shouldn't do that!" I scolded. I regretted my outburst immediately. "Sorry!" I said as her face crumpled. "You made me jump. It always make me feel cross."

She pursed her lips.

"I'm sorry, Aunt Bea!"

"Never mind. Now, tell me. Who will be devastated?"

I stood to the side allowing her to see the bird on the doorstep.

"Oh, dear! The poor bird." Straightening, she turned to me with surprising composure. "This is the work of that murderous witch. It is a warning. She knows we're on to her." Lips pursed and eyes narrowed, she ushered me inside then closed the door. Her aura had brightened but held a dark tinge close to her figure. Aunt Beatrice was a petite but formidable force of energy and I felt her anger as waves. "We must inform Loveday immediately. This has gone too far. Trespassing on Haligern land and now threatening us at our front door. We must take action."

"But what about Thomasin? She will be devastated!"

"She will be filled with righteous anger and a need for revenge. Oh, that poisonous witch doesn't know what she has taken on. When she feels our wrath, then she will truly know what it means to cross Haligern Coven!"

I had never seen my aunt so animated by anger.

"But ... don't you think Thomasin should be told?"

"Of course. Euphemia also. We must begin anew with our efforts. We must thwart this dark magick and restore Haligern's strength."

"Yes, but Aunt Thomasin-"

"Thomasin. Thomasin. Thomasin. Whatever has gotten into you, Livitha? It is Loveday and Raif who are being attacked. Their lives that are in danger. Why are you going on about Thomasin?"

Scalded by her ire, my cheeks flushed. "Well ... it's just that Benny ..." I gestured to the bird stiffening on the step.

Aunt Beatrice considered me for a moment. "Tsk! .... Oh, Livitha! Did you think that poor bird was Benny?" She held my gaze as I nodded then slipped an arm around my waist. "Poor, poor girl. You must feel terrible. No. Benny is in the kitchen. I've just scolded him for wirriting Bess, although I think she was enjoying the attention."

"So! Benny's not dead?"

"No!" she laughed and squeezed my waist. "No. Come see."

I followed her through to the kitchen just in time to see Benny hop down onto Bess's back. The whippet yelped and began to chase her tail. Lucifer was curled beside the hearth, feigning sleep.

"You could have told me, Lucifer!" I chided.

"Oh, don't blame old Lou. He must have gotten distracted by the saucer of port I put out for him."

At this he fixed huge, green, and accusing eyes on Aunt Beatrice. "Less of the 'old', if you don't mind!"

Ignoring Lucifer's reprimand, I held out my hand for Benny. Large claws gripped my fingers and he considered me with a beady eye. I stroked his raven black head then promised to dig him some worms from the garden. This seemed to please him, and he nodded his head, eyes glinting.

Lucifer huffed in the corner. "I suppose I shall have to play dead to receive the same treatment!"

"Oh, Lucifer!" I said with a laugh. "You know I love you!"

"Pah!" he retorted and closed his eyes, tucking his tail tight around him with a disparaging flick.

"Sit down, dear," Aunt Beatrice said. She clicked her fingers and flames leapt within the stove's oven. Lucifer hissed, but quickly returned to sleep. "You've had a shock this morning. I can feel your energy—it is so ... grating."

"Oh," I said. "You're right. I do feel on edge."

"Well, a nice cup of tea and a few drops of Euphemia's special elixir will do you the world of good."

I sat contemplating the garden as Aunt Beatrice bustled in the kitchen, trilling a tune as she placed the kettle on the stove and placed a teacup and saucer on the table for me. It took me back to my childhood and I let the feeling of comfort envelope me as Aunt Beatrice continued her gentle, arcane, tune. Fractious energy that had begun to tingle in my fingertips ebbed and, as I sipped my tea laced with a calmative, I relaxed. Thoughts that had been so jumbled and fraught began to flow at a smoother rate, exploring and connecting ideas.

We weren't getting anywhere on our own. We needed help. As I took another sip of tea, mulling the idea of just who we should ask for help, Aunt Beatrice stopped sweeping the floor, placed a hand on her hip and said, "I know just what we have to do."

"You do?"

"Yes, we have to visit the *Council of Witches*. Those old crones owe us and it's time to call in the favour!"

Chapter Fourteen

It was decided that I would drive Aunt Thomasin and Aunt Beatrice to the Council's office whilst Aunt Euphemia stayed behind to take care of Aunt Loveday and Uncle Raif. With Mrs. Driscoll at the cottage too, I felt confident that they were in capable hands.

We set off and, as we emerged from the tree-lined and narrow driveway that led to the road, I realised I had no idea where we were going.

"I'll need directions." I glanced in the rear-view mirror. Both aunts had taken the backseat leaving me to feel something like a chauffeur.

"Oh. Well, I haven't thought about directions," said Aunt Beatrice. "Have you, Thomasin?"

Silence for a moment was followed by, "No. They hadn't crossed my mind."

I continued to drive and when comment wasn't forthcoming, said, "So ... are you going to tell me where to drive to?"

"Well ..."

"I think ..."

"Please tell me you know where it is."

"Of course we do!"

"Yes! We do!"

By this time, we had reached the junction where I would ordinarily take the right in order to go into the village. I indicated then pulled out.

"No! Stop! The other way." Aunt Beatrice shouted.

Startled, I braked and managed to stall the car. Both aunts jolted forward.

"Sorry!"

Thankfully, there were no other cars on the road, and I managed to change direction without issue, but as soon as I came to a passing place, I pulled over.

"I can't drive all the way to the Council offices like this! My nerves will be shattered."

"Well, what do you suggest?"

"I suggest that you tell me where we're going so that I can punch the details into the Sat Nav-"

"We witches don't need ... Sat Navs!"

"Fine, but unless you both want to fly there, I suggest you let me know where we're going so that I can drive us there—safely!" I realised that I was being a little sharp, but there was no way I could drive 'blind' to the Council with only last minute and muddled instructions from one of my aunts.

"Well, let's see," Aunt Beatrice closed her eyes and then said, "Yes. The nearest village is Goxhill. From there I know the route but I'm not sure of the names of the roads. It's not very easy to find."

Aunt Thomasin cackled. "No, not very easy at all."

I punched Goxhill into the Sat Nav and was rewarded with directions. "It's ninety-two miles away!" I said with dismay.

"Broom flight would be easier?" suggested Aunt Thomasin.

"Tssk! Now, you know we can't do that. At least not in daylight."

"So many rules! I do find them tiresome."

"It's *The Gathering* soon. You can let off some steam then."

With my aunts now reminiscing about past Gatherings, I pulled back onto the road. It would take hours before we arrived at Goxhill. I put my foot down and followed the Sat Nav's soothing voice.

My hope of the journey taking a couple of hours was misplaced. It was nearly three before we arrived at the village and then another twenty minutes passed before we found the road that led to the Council office.

"Where is that entrance?" Aunt Thomasin said as we drove along the narrow country lane where they insisted the Witch Council office was located.

I realised then that, to my knowledge, no one had called ahead to check that someone would actually be at the office. "Um, will they be expecting us?"

"Oh, yes. They know we're coming."

"But you didn't say anything about calling them."

"Don't fret, Livitha. I'm sure someone will be there. There's always someone there. Isn't that right, Thomasin."

"Well, I suppose so. Although you never know what those cantankerous old crones are getting up to."

"So, you haven't called them?"

"No, but someone is always there."

I held back a sigh of frustration. Hours of continuous driving had given me a headache and I was already losing the will to continue. If the journey had all been for nothing!

"Livitha, calm down. They will be there," soothed Aunt Beatrice having once again read my thoughts.

"Fine," I sighed.

To my dismay, we reached the end of the narrow road. Beyond, the land opened out to rolling hills where sheep grazed beneath billowing clouds that cast dark shadows.

"So where is it?"

"We've missed it!"

"How can we have missed it?" I asked, exasperation rising.

"Well, it's very well hidden."

"Those old crones are so paranoid they make it impossible for even witches to find!"

"They do it on purpose. They don't like to be bothered."

We drove back down the lane and had reached the halfway point when Aunt Beatrice became animated. "There it is!" She tapped a finger against the window. "There. Do you see the sign? Slow down, Livitha. You're going to miss it."

I slowed to a stop. To the left was a narrow gap between a hedge of overgrown hawthorn. To one side, several feet back and camouflaged among the leaves was a sign.

"It's an old RAF base," I said. "Probably from the second World War."

"The US Air Force were also stationed here. But you're right, it is an old airfield."

"In we go then!"

"The gap is too narrow. I can't get the car down there!"

"Fiddlesticks. Of course you can."

I considered the narrow gap. It was only about three feet wide. "I can assure you that I can't."

"Trust me, Livitha, when I say that you can. Now put your foot down on that pedal and motor forward, please."

I hesitated.

"Go on then," Aunt Beatrice nagged.

"Fine! I will."

Fully expecting the car to get wedged between the trees, or at the very least scratched, I drove forward, gripping the wheel with white knuckles and hunched shoulders as I approached the narrow gap. As the front bumper touched the tree, the leaves and branches shrank, widening the gap, and I lurched through to the other side. Beyond was an area of overgrown scrubland. At its centre sat a derelict Nissen hut, the curve of its corrugated roof overhung with trees. A grime-smeared window sat to the side of a narrow door with a rotting, now slanted, door frame.

"Are you sure this is it?" I asked as I slowed the car to a stop in front of the derelict building.

"You'll see!"

After parking the car, and stepping out into the sunshine, it became clear that no one had visited for years. The place was derelict.

As we stood in front of the hut, Aunt Thomasin said, "Now, listen carefully, Livitha. There are words you must say upon entering and again upon leaving. The first will let you in, the second will let you out, but you must pronounce them properly or you'll get trapped, particularly on the way out—the magick is very mischievous and loves to cause us trouble!"

I glanced at the grimy window and shivered. "Okay. Can we practice first?"

"No, you must just repeat what I say."

"There's no need to worry. Just repeat exactly what we say, as we say it."

"And if you do get trapped ... No. You won't, so don't worry."

Perturbed, I stood with my aunts, and put all my effort into repeating their magical words. As we finished, the air in front of the Nissen hut shimmered and the façade of decay fell away. The hut remained but was now in pristine condition. The brickwork front looked freshly built, the door was shiny with black gloss paint, and the window, beneath which hung a manger-style basket of brightly coloured flowers, gleamed. Several cars were parked to the side and smoke rose in a twist from the chimney in its arched roof. A tree, heavy with ripe apples, sat to one side.

"Oh, that's lovely!"

"It's just as nice inside. The old crones know how to make themselves comfortable."

"They always have," agreed Aunt Beatrice.

Chapter Fifteen

The Nissen hut didn't become Tardis-like as I stepped inside. The dimensions were what you would expect of the hut. It appeared to be at least twenty feet wide and nearly forty feet long. The first ten feet or so were given over to a reception area laid with well-worn oak floorboards. Either side, floor-to-ceiling shelves were packed with books, many of them leather bound and ancient, others with modern paper or hardback covers. A waist-height, gated partition sat across the width of the hut, behind it were several desks, each piled with books. Beyond the desks were two emerald-green velvet sofas. This area was lit by lamplight and between them was a coffee table, again piled with books and several coffee mugs.

Halfway along one side, a stone-built fireplace, that would have looked more at home in a primitive country home, dominated. This section of the room was filled with open shelves stocked with jars and potion bottles and hung with drying herbs. There were also two huge and ancient pantry-like lockable cupboards each with a large iron key in their keyholes. A cauldron hung from an iron hook within the chimney and a woman stood before it with a huge ladle. She turned to us as we entered. Behind her, three women seated on the sofas looked up from their books. One held a Kindle and clapped the cover closed.

"'Tis the Haligern coven, sisters!" the woman at the cauldron called down to the women at the end of the hut.

"I knew it! I told you they were coming."

"As did I!"

"I dreamt it last night."

"I saw it foretold in the fire yesterday afternoon."

Aunt Thomasin allowed a low groan to escape.

"Hst!" Aunt Beatrice dug a surreptitious elbow into her side.

I recognised the woman at the cauldron as Anne Whittle, a witch who had attended my Initiation ceremony. She had drunk several cocktails too many whilst chatting in the kitchen and had to be carried out to the car at the end of the evening. She raised the ladle and waved it at us.

As the other women approached, I recognised them too. They had also been drinking cocktails in the kitchen during the party. Tempers had flared between them as they argued who was to be the designated driver and the issue had only been settled when Bessie Yickar and Janet Horne had downed several cocktails in quick succession so forcing Margaret Pringle to remain sober. Sitting with them was a younger woman I didn't recognise. She was on the plump side but curvaceous with dark, glossy hair worn in a messy chignon. With her tight jeans accentuating a full but curvaceous figure, high heels, and fitted top she looked nothing like my aunts or the other witches in the room. She threw me a friendly smile from over the top of glasses perched on her nose. I liked her immediately.

"Sisters!" Bessie Yickar enthused. "We're so glad you're here, and not a little too soon. We have a surprise for you."

"We have one for you," Aunt Thomasin said with less enthusiasm.

"Oh? Well, ours first!"

She grabbed hold of the dark-haired woman's elbow. "This is Effemia. We call her Effie for short. She's our newest recruit. She's a direct descendant of Frioðulf."

I had no idea who Frioðulf was or his/her significance, but guessed he was probably a contemporary of my aunts.

"He was a king of Lindsey," Aunt Beatrice clarified.

"Yes, he was. Oh, those were the days!"

Despite knowing that my aunts were centuries old, I was surprised at her words. Unlike my aunts, Bessie looked no more than sixty, and a very well-maintained sixty too.

Effemia stepped forward, obviously a little uncomfortable being the centre of attention. "Hi! It's nice to meet you."

"A new recruit?" Aunt Beatrice queried.

"Yes! She's training as a Vardlokkur."

"A warlock?"

Bessie nodded with excitement. "Yes! Isn't it marvellous! After all this time, we have a new vardlokkur. Obviously, she has to go through an apprenticeship, but well ..."

"She's something of an amateur sleuth too," Margaret Pringle said.

The other women nodded with pride.

"Yes! She's solved one of our cold cases!"

I was instantly intrigued. This was something we both had in common. Perhaps we could exchange numbers. I flashed her a smile. She could be a friend I didn't need to hide my true self from!

"Livitha is something of an amateur detective too," Aunt Beatrice added, not to be outdone.

"Oh?" Bessie Yickar's question was something of a challenge.

"Yes, she discovered who killed her husband's mistress-"

"Aunt Bea-"

"And helped stop a serial killer!" Aunt Beatrice continued in triumph.

"Well!" Bessie said with poorly hidden envy. "That is wonderful, I must say."

"It is," Aunt Beatrice agreed. The tension between the women rose and I could feel the crackle of the embers of a fractious energy. Despite the smiles I knew there was a difficult history between the women.

"And so is discovering a new vardlokkur, Bessie," Aunt Thomasin said with Loveday-like diplomacy. "You must tell us all about it."

Bessie gazed at Effemia as if in wonder then sighed. "It's just so wonderful. So much like the old days. I was so much looking forward to surprising you all at *The Gathering*, but you've beaten me to it."

"Stop prattling, Bessie!" An older witch with a band of thick white hair framing her face stepped forward. She opened the partition gate and ushered us through. "Come and sit down. Effie will make coffee whilst we speak.

Effemia disappeared through a door at the end of the hut whilst we were guided to the velvet sofas. Once we were seated, Janet blurted, "I have been sensing much trouble recently. A terrible fear about Loveday."

The other women nodded.

"We have noticed a change."

"Loveday is the very reason why we are here," Aunt Thomasin explained.

"She's being murdered!" Aunt Beatrice cried out, unable to hold back her emotion. "Murdered by a witch!"

"What?"

"Yes! And a witch using dark, dark magick."

"We have found a death-bringing gallows on Haligern land," Aunt Thomasin explained.

"And Loveday is nearly dead!"

"Dead!"

"Yes! And Raif too!"

"No! Not Raif!"

"Hush now, sister. Calm yourself. Becoming overwrought is the last thing we need."

The next minutes were spent recounting Uncle Raif's and Aunt Loveday's declining health, as well as how Aggie Sampson had aged, the continuing dilapidation of Haligern, and the black magick paraphernalia we had found circling the cottage.

"I am shocked," Janet declared. "The death-bringing gallows were outlawed centuries ago."

"That's right! They were," said Bessie, "and I remember the reason why. Do you remember?"

Aunt's Thomasin and Beatrice shook their heads.

Bessie glanced at the Council witches and shivered. "Effemia, bring me the book."

"Book?"

"Yes, yes! The Book of Records. It's in the library."

Effemia unlocked one of the large pantry-like cupboards, stepped inside, and disappeared.

"She's gone!" I whispered to Aunt Beatrice.

"She'll be back shortly."

Several minutes passed without Effemia returning.

"It's on the desk, to the left," called Bessie helpfully.

Seconds later Effemia called a triumphant, 'Got it!' and stepped out of the cupboard, dusting cobwebs from her shoulder.

Itching with curiosity about the impossibly deep cupboard, I forced myself to remain seated. The book, a large leather-bound tome, was placed on the table in front of Bessie. She opened the book and leafed through it.

"Hah! Yes, here it is," she said and swivelled the book around for us to see, stabbing her finger at an entry written in black ink in an archaic script. "See. 'Hegelina Fekkitt sentenced to 'bewrece'. See the date, 1754. She was exiled for use of the 'forlædan deáþbeám', the death-bringing tree. She turned the book to face her and continued to read. "She was banished for ... two hundred and sixty-seven years. Effemia, pass me my mobile. Gilly will know."

"Gilly Duncan," Aunt Thomasin explained. "She's the head of Intra-realm Security."

"Oh," I said as though it all made sense then listened as, mobile to her ear, Bessie asked to speak to Gilly Duncan then paced the room. After several minutes of questioning, she turned to us. "Ladies, it seems that Hegelina was paroled two months ago. She's out under a conditional licence."

"So ... you think it could be her that's poisoning Aunt Loveday?"

Bessie nodded, her countenance grave. "Loveday and Aggie Sampson were on the panel that found Hegelina guilty and sentenced her to a period of hard labour and then exile.

All the pieces slotted together. "It's her! She did it!" I said with utter conviction. "Where can we find her?"

"That's the problem. She hasn't reported to her parole officer for the last month and no one has been able to find her."

"Do you have a photograph?"

"Photograph? She has been in the other realm for more than two hundred years. There are no photographs."

"A painting then? An image?"

"Oh, yes!" said Janet. "She featured in a book. Cotta's *Trial of Witchcraft*."

A cold chill ran through me. "John Cotta?"

"Yes, that's right. Are you familiar with his work?"

Aunt Beatrice coughed. Aunt Thomasin made an odd squeaking noise.

"No! Of course she's not," Aunt Thomasin said. "How could she? She is only a novitiate and hasn't even been presented at the *Gathering*."

"Ah, yes, of course. Well, that is something to look forward to. I do enjoy a good cocktail and a dance around the fire."

"Yes, it will be a wonderful evening, sister," Aunt Thomasin agreed. "Now, we must get back to Loveday and tell her the news."

"But where are we going to find Hegelina?" I asked.

"Do not worry, sisters," Bessie replied. "We shall make enquiries and with Effie on the case it shall be solved in no time."

Aunt Beatrice stiffened. "I'm sure Livitha doesn't need help," she said archly. "After all, it is she who trapped a serial killer only a few weeks ago."

Taken aback, Bessie's brow arched.

Aunt Thomasin tugged at Beatrice's elbow. "We appreciate any help and, of course, if Effemia can discover any information that will help us save Loveday, we will gladly accept it. Won't we Beatrice!"

Aunt Beatrice offered a begrudging, "Yes."

Chapter Sixteen

Back in the car I wanted to know everything about Dr. Cotta.

"Who is John Cotta?"

"Tsk!" berated Aunt Beatrice still cranky from her confrontation with Bessie. "We haven't time for this."

"I can talk whilst I drive."

"You know you're not very good at talking and doing, dear. I'd rather that you concentrated on the road."

Ahead I spotted a passing place and pulled into it.

"Tell me who he is. It's obvious that you all know about him. You've made it quite clear that you don't approve of me going to dinner with him. So, what exactly is wrong with him?"

"He's a Cotta."

"Yes, I know that, but the doctor who wrote that book, isn't the same person as the doctor."

"That's what he tells you."

I shook my head. "The original Doctor Cotta lived hundreds of years ago. He's dead. My Doctor Cotta is his great-great-great nephew, and then some. Are you trying to tell me they are the same person? Is he a witch too?"

"Pah! A witch? Never."

"And he's not the same man," Aunt Thomasin clarified.

"Then why are you all so dead set against him?"

"Well, you said yourself that he was so enamoured by his ancestor that he was following in his footsteps. The very reason he is in England is to study his work and visit his birthplace. Is that not correct?"

"Yes, but that's because his great-great-great-great uncle – or whatever - was a doctor who believed in science. He was working against quackery and advocating the training of doctors. He wanted them to take science seriously and use it in medicine."

"He also believed in witches."

"Okay," I said a little taken aback. "But that's not a bad thing. Is it?"

"Matthew Hopkins also believed in witches."

Another cold chill ran through me. "The Witchfinder General." I said quietly, my fingers remembering the pain he inflicted upon them. "Are you saying that the original Doctor Cotta was a witchfinder?"

"His work was used to justify our persecution, torture, and death."

"The book Bessie Yickar referred to was actually given the title, *The Trial of Witchcraft Showing the True and Right Method of Discovery*, or something like that.

"So, he was using science to discover witches?"

"Well, no, he was disputing what he saw as erroneous ways of proving witchcraft."

"Livitha, he was a leading expert in his day, and was determined to uncover our secrets. We try so hard to remain under the radar as they say, but John Cotta helped to convince people of our existence. There were those who were beginning to deny that we did."

"Yes, he even argued that an eyewitness account was sufficient to charge a person with witchcraft."

"Well, I suppose that meant he thought torture was wrong?" I ventured.

"Well ... that's beside the point."

"Is it?"

"The man believed in witches. Of course, he was right-"

"We've done everything in our power to reverse the damage since then."

"And have succeeded—to a large extent."

"But he confirmed to a populace that feared us that we did exist. Although he argued against our torture as a means of gaining confession-"

"So, he was a good person?"

My aunts were silent.

"I can't say that he was."

"We can't say that he wasn't. But by insisting that we existed, he only helped fuel the witch hunts."

I fell silent. The trauma of the witch hunts was as real in my aunts' memories as though they had happened yesterday. I could understand their point.

"Dr. Cotta collects the books," I stated. "I'll ask him if I can take a look and try to find the image of Hegelina."

"Yes, that's a good idea."

"And then perhaps you can cut the ties that bind, dear."

"Well ..."

"It's for the best. You can never trust a Cotta."

I shook my head. I understood their attitude towards the doctor, but felt their suspicion was ultimately mistaken. After all, he was merely a relative of the original doctor and only interested in his family's history, not in perpetuating the persecution of witches.

"I'll go to him tonight. Once I've dropped you off at the cottage."

"Good girl."

After our return to Haligern, and after checking in on Raif and Loveday and putting my mind at rest that they were still alive, I made my way back to the village and Dr. Cotta's surgery. By the time I arrived the sun was casting long shadows in the courtyard. As I stood at the door, fist raised ready to knock I realised I hadn't called ahead. I was arriving unannounced! An unforgiveable faux pas!

I hovered for a moment, toyed with the idea of returning to my car and calling to arrange a time that would be convenient for him but, just as I turned to leave, the door opened. Concern was etched upon Dr. Cotta's face. "Liv! Is everything alright?"

"Yes! Sorry! I didn't mean to turn up unannounced." I scrambled to think of an excuse. I couldn't tell him the truth that I wanted to look through his books to check an image of a witch made several hundred years old. I decided to lie. I wasn't proud of myself. "Hi! Yes. I was just passing and ... thought perhaps you'd like some company." My left brow twitched as my fingertips fizzed with the pain of supercharged pins and needles. I was literally inviting myself round. I was completely out of my comfort zone.

With a bemused frown he checked behind him into the hall.

He must have a guest! "Sorry! If you're busy ..." I said. Heat singed my cheeks. I wasn't welcome! My resolve to nose through his books faltered. "I'll go. Another time ..."

"No! I mean, it's fine. Please. Come in."

"Well, only if you're sure. I don't want to interrupt you."

"You're not. I was just reading ... doing a bit of research, but a break would be good. And you know I enjoy your company." He threw me a dazzling smile.

I was a little taken aback by the friendliness of his smile and guilt nagged me. I was being duplicitous, using his desire to be my friend to suit my own needs. I was being sly, a user, and it didn't suit me well. I promised myself that I'd make it up to him with a nice evening out, perhaps another meal at the *Imaginarium* once I'd dealt with the hex that was poisoning Aunt Loveday. Of course, that would mean deceiving my aunts! "Thanks!" I replied, my cheeks burning hot.

He stepped back to allow me in then led the way to the kitchen. The door to his study was open, an angle lamp illuminated a book and a small contraption threaded with wires. As I passed the room a red light switched off and a yellow one flashed.

In the kitchen Dr. Cotta offered me a glass of red wine which I declined as I was driving. I accepted tea and whilst the kettle boiled, I made clumsy efforts to engage him in conversation about his books and specifically about his ancestor, the infamous seventeenth-century John Cotta. "When I was here before, you promised to show me your books. I didn't take you up on that offer."

"Well, I guess they're just dry and dusty old things." He said with his back still to me. I was surprised at his change of attitude; he had been so enthusiastic before.

"I'd love to know more about your great, great ... great uncle Cotta." I decided to be bold. Aunt Loveday was running out of time. "I'd love to have a look at his books. I've always loved history and the sixteenth century has always fascinated me."

"He wrote during the seventeenth century." He caught my gaze. "Both centuries were full of witches."

Our eyes locked for a moment before I broke from his gaze. "Yes, I guess they were," I said, trying to hide my surprise at his statement.

"There were many, but more were accused than had any kind of supernatural, devil-given power."

"Devil given?"

"That's what they thought. That a witch's power came from the devil—a pact with Satan."

My fingers itched as he continued.

"But in the main, the accusations of witchcraft was spurious, just one neighbour looking for a bit of vengeance on another. One uneducated soul accusing another of causing harm. A disagreement often caused by an unfortunate co-incidence."

"Yep!" I said trying to quelle my nerves as Dr. Cotta smiled. He seemed to be watching me carefully.

"I'm guessing that's why you're interested in my ancestor," he smiled. "You think he was some kind of witchfinder?"

"A witchfinder! No! You said he was a doctor—some sort of progressive."

Dr. Cotta smiled. "He was. He insisted that medicine be grounded in science and not just superstition and guesswork. It's what I admire about him, but even he believed in witches." He paused. "So, do you really want to look at my books?"

"Yes."

"This way." He threw one of his dazzling smiles and I followed him through to the study.

On the table a desk lamp shone down upon the small black box. The light on its top shone green. Dr. Cotta reached for a book from the table and, as I stepped forward to take it, the light on the box began to flash yellow. I noticed that the book on the table was open to a page of diagrams and mathematical symbols. It reminded me of textbooks from 'O' Level physics, an exam which I had failed miserably.

"This is interesting," I said gesturing to the contraption on the table. As I stepped closer to get a better look, the yellow light intensified and changed from flashing to solid.

Dr. Cotta made an odd noise in his throat. "Are you alright?" I asked as he grasped the back of his chair. He could only gurgle and nod. Confused by his behaviour, I stepped back from the desk. The yellow light dimmed and once again began to flash. Dr. Cotta stared from me to the light, then stared across the room and made a fuss about finding another of John Cotta's books. Whilst he searched the bookshelves, I stepped to the contraption and away several times to test my theory. Each time I stepped close, the yellow light grew bright and solid. When I stepped away it dimmed and flashed. It was reacting to me!

As Dr. Cotta stepped beside me, I moved away on the pretext of turning on the main light. The light dimmed despite Dr. Cotta standing beside the contraption. It was *only* responding to me. The hairs on the back of my neck stood on end. What was this device?

The energy in the room was fractious and with my anxiety growing I checked through the book. There were only two images. The first was a woodcut printed as the frontispiece and the second depicted a courtroom. A woman stood accused of witchcraft, a black mark on her arm labelled as 'Satan's marke', but the features were too indistinct to be useful. Thinking that a book from the seventeenth century would hold a realistic image of the witch I was hunting, was proof of my desperation for clues.

"So," I said, holding the book with care. "Your uncle was part of the witch hunts? Did he know ... Matthew Hopkins?"

Dr. Cotta frowned and then shook his head. "No. Hopkins wasn't born when my uncle wrote his books."

"But he was part of the witch trials?"

"No, although he did believe in witches, and stated as much in his books. But they were used as justification for the witch hunts."

I placed the book on the table. The yellow light grew bright. Dr. Cotta made a sucking noise with his lips. It was obvious that the light brightening had an effect on him.

"What is that?" I pointed at the contraption. The light became solid.

Dr. Cotta looked from the yellow light to me. "It's a ... It's a prototype."

"A prototype of what?"

"... A radio."

"A radio?"

"Yep."

"So why does the light brighten up when I get close?"

I tested the light, putting my hand close, then pulled it away. It grew bright then dimmed.

"It can detect your energy."

"But it's a radio. How can it detect my energy?"

"It ..."

"It doesn't do it to you!" I was genuinely interested.

"Well ... I guess my energy's not as strong as yours."

This explanation made no sense to me, but I was almost devoid of knowledge about physics. Plus, Dr. Cotta's reaction was one of barely contained excitement. He looked pained at the effort of holding his tongue.

"It's not a radio, is it."

"Kind of ... it picks up frequencies."

"But not radio frequencies, like FM or AM or whatever."

"No," he agreed.

"So, what is it?"

He was silent for a moment and then, with a huge grin, blurted. "It's a witch detector. My uncle insisted that there were witches, yet he was a scientific man, he knew, and I had to prove him right. And I have!"

"You think I'm a witch!" I blurted.

"I know you are."

Chapter Seventeen

With every sense tingling and my inner core superheating, a tremble ran through my arms to my fingers. I was trapped by Dr. Cotta's gaze like a rabbit caught in headlights. I couldn't give the slightest hint that he was right. After uncomfortable seconds of silence, and with my fingertips fizzing, and an almost irresistible need to send a bolt of destructive energy at the flashing contraption on the table, I burst into laughter.

"A witch? Me?"

He nodded. "Erm ... yes!"

I continued to laugh, trying my best to seem natural. "Funny! I've been called a few things in my life, but never a witch."

"You and your aunts-"

I decided that pulling the offended card was by best hope of defence. "My aunts?" I asked allowing the smile on my face to slip.

"Yes, I expect they're witches too. You've got a real, bona-fide coven at Haligern Cottage."

I shook my head. "This joke is going a little too far. You can't be serious."

"I am," he said with deadly earnest.

"Then I'm not sure what to say other than I think your great uncle's books are giving you some odd ideas. Everyone knows there are no such things as witches."

"There are!"

I shook my head again. "Listen, I'm not sure what you're trying to achieve, but I don't take kindly to being accused of being a witch. It's just silly!"

"Well, we'll see about that."

The atmosphere became increasingly tense, and I had a sudden desire to run. "It's getting late. I'm sorry to have bothered you, but I really must go now."

He continued to watch me closely and, for a moment, I thought leaving might become an issue, but he simply nodded and walked me to the door. I remained polite and thanked him for allowing me to see his books and threw a final bemused smile as I left. Whether he believed in my innocence or not I couldn't tell, but I raced home with trembling hands and a pounding heart. He had a witch detector! And it worked. How could we keep our witchy status a secret now?

Back at the cottage I found Aunts Beatrice, Thomasin, and Euphemia in the kitchen. Loveday had retired early after a tiring day. I wasted no time in filling them in on what I had discovered in the book – the woodcut showing a witch on trial, her features indistinct but with a dark patch on her arm.

"It could be her. If I remember rightly, she did have a large patch of dark skin on her arm. It was a mole, but they claimed that it was a witch mark. That it resembled a horned creature didn't help. Very silly, but then, that is what they believed back then."

"She was convicted?"

"Yes, but she managed to escape. I know there was a terrible scandal about it at the time. She managed to use her powers to convince them that her cellmate was her and the poor woman was executed instead. The truth was only obvious as she hung, and the 'glamour' wore off."

"Poor woman!"

"She was. Poor lady had six children and had been wrongly accused—a malicious accusation among neighbours as so many accusations of witchcraft were in those days. Her accuser had a change of heart and she was going to be released that morning. Unfortunately, for her, and her children, the goal's administrative system was Kafkaesque in those days."

"An innocent died because of Hegelina."

"What became of the children?"

"Their father had died in the months before, so they were orphaned. It was decided by the Council that they would be supported by the local coven, as a way of making amends. Hegelina was a witch after all. She *was* guilty of their crime of witchcraft, but did she deserve to be hung? No! But replacing herself with an innocent, now that was unforgiveable."

"Indeed."

"And that's what got her banished?"

"No."

"No?"

"It was using the death tree several decades later, that finally brought her downfall among the covens."

"And Loveday was on the Council when the decision was made."

"Yes. And Aggie Sampson too."

I nodded. "It fits. It's what links them both. There's a clear motive—if revenge is the goal."

I fidgeted on my chair.

"Livitha, what is it? There's something else to tell."

I nodded, then poured out my horror at discovering Dr. Cotta's witch-detecting device.

"Didn't you destroy it?"

"No, how could I? It was sat on the table right in front of him."

"It must be destroyed."

"You could have used a spell to break it."

"I was flustered. It was a struggle to respond without admitting I was a witch."

"We'll have to take action sisters. A contraption to capture witches-"

"He didn't say it was a contraption to capture witches," I said in Dr. Cotta's defence, "only that it detected witches."

"Well, it *will* be used to capture witches!"

"Now, now. Let us all remain calm. Our priority has to be helping break the hex that is poisoning Loveday."

"How is she?"

"Our spells and charms seem to be helping. She has a little more energy and has only just gone up to bed."

"And Uncle Raif."

"Yes, he too seems improved."

I breathed a sigh of relief. "So, what next?"

"Well, we continue to use our own magick as an antidote to the hex and make our best efforts to find Hegelina."

"And go to Lady Heskitt's wedding."

"Oh, the wedding! I keep forgetting about it. Do we really have to go?"

"Yes-"

"But Loveday and Raif-"

"Loveday and Raif will be absolutely fine!"

I turned with surprise. Aunt Loveday stood in the doorway.

"I insist that you go," she said. "Afterall, it's only one evening and the change will do you good. You all need some relaxation."

"I'm not sure going to Lady Heskitt's wedding will help me relax," I complained. "I have nothing to wear, my hair is a mess, I haven't had my nails done and I'm sure everyone there will be gorgeous and slim and perfectly manicured and coiffured."

"You'll look lovely, Livitha. Stop being so negative about yourself," Aunt Euphemia chided. "You're a very pretty woman."

"She has a lot of admirers!"

"I don't think Dr. Cotta's interest in me was for that reason. The more I think about it, the more convinced I am that he was trying to discover more about the coven. There were several times during our conversations when he would ask questions about you all."

"You were circumspect?"

"Always."

"You were careful of the choice of your words?"

"Yes."

"Then you have nothing to worry about."

"Well, apart from his witch-detecting contraption!"

"What witch detecting contraption?"

Aunt Loveday hadn't heard our previous conversation and I spent the next minutes explaining exactly what I had seen and what Dr. Cotta had said about his device to detect witches. She sagged in her chair and shook her head.

"Oh, dear! We really must do something about that!"

"Indeed."

"As soon as possible."

She nodded. "We will deal with it the day after the wedding."

Communal murmurs of assent passed between my aunts.

"Until then, let us rest."

Aunt Loveday rose, said goodnight, and disappeared upstairs. I doubted she would have a restful night.

The following day passed slowly. I managed to organise an outfit before I left for the shop and, over breakfast, we agreed to ask Mrs. Driscoll to come round and sit with Loveday and Raif for the evening. She had readily agreed on the condition we tell her all the details about the ceremony, and gossip about the guests, over elevenses the next morning.

Chapter Eighteen

By the time it was time to leave for the wedding the following evening, all unsightly hairs had been plucked, and I was perfumed, painted, and coiffured to the best of my ability. Dressed in a flattering wrap-over dress that somehow gave me a waist, topped by a mink stole complete with diamond clasp borrowed from Aunt Euphemia, and a hat with a tiny veil from Aunt Thomasin, both of which dated from the nineteen forties, we sat in the car with thirty minutes to spare. The car was immaculate, although I noticed that the chrome casing around the headlights were pitted, and the paintwork a little dull and faded in places. It chugged as Aunt Thomasin started the engine.

"Oh, dear!" She moved the gears into first and released the clutch. It moved forward with a grinding jerk then stalled.

Concerned and murmured foreboding filled the car.

"We'd best take my car," I said.

Aunt Beatrice sighed. "I think we shall, Livitha." A note of emotion trembled in her voice.

The air was heavy with distraught energy. All my life my aunts had cared for me but in that moment, I knew it was my turn to care for them. I turned to the back seat and regarded each for a moment. Each aunt looked just as she always did – radiant despite their frowns of concern. Whatever poisonous magick was afflicting Aunt Loveday wasn't affecting them. At least it didn't seem that way. However, I was filled with determination to be their strength that evening. For a change, I wouldn't be the one crumbling, a whirl of chaotic hormones. I would show a stiff upper lip, embrace the challenge, and lift the energy that enveloped us.

"Right!" I said, taking charge.

The car grew silent. I had their attention.

"We are not going to wallow in this. Tonight, we are going to enjoy ourselves!"

"But how can we enjoy ourselves when Loveday and Raif are so sick?"

I held Aunt Thomasin's gaze. "They wouldn't want us moping."

"That's true. Loveday would school us to be careful of our words and then demand that we enjoy the evening."

"That's exactly what she said when I took her supper through," said Aunt Euphemia.

"I think that Hegelina wants us to crumble and fall into ruin along with the house. Well! I refuse. I refuse to be her victim. So, we shall watch Lady Heskitt marry beneath the stars, toast the happy couple with a glass of champagne-"

"Will there be dancing. I love to dance."

"Oh, yes! I'd love to dance. I haven't danced in such a long time."

Aunt Beatrice's eyes glittered. "Will your young man be there, Livitha?"

"My young man?"

"Which one?" Aunt Thomasin tittered. "She has several to choose from."

For a moment I wished I hadn't tried to raise their spirits. I was the object of their mirth once again.

"Ooh! Which one would you choose Thomasin?"

"Well ... not Pascal!"

"Ugh! Philandering toad!"

"Adulterous scoundrel!"

"Just a minute-."

"Although he was quite handsome in his younger days."

All three aunts tittered.

"Now just wait a minute-"

"Hmm!" continued Thomasin ignoring my indignation. "Well ... who would it be? Blackwood or Cotta?"

"Ooh! Cotta! Definitely. He is so, so handsome. Such a catch."

"I agree. A bronzed god. So much like Thor in that film."

"But Blackwood has that dark and brooding element and something just a little dangerous."

"And broad shoulders."

"Narrow hips."

"A pert bottom despite his age."

"Aunt Bea!"

I made another attempt to intervene, but they were oblivious to me. Cheeks burning, I left their car to an outburst of amused cackling.

Several minutes later, cheeks flushed, they joined me in my car. As we rolled through the gates they began to giggle. I let out a martyred sigh but couldn't help smiling. They were happy and that was more than I could expect given the circumstances.

Chapter Nineteen

Heskitt Hall lay deep within Heskitt land and, after turning off the main road, and then following a narrow country road banked either side by ancient and overhanging trees, the entrance to the estate was announced by imposing brick pillars and a huge and decorative iron gate. On the other side of the brick pillars was an attractive gatehouse, a single storey construction of decorative brickwork and patterned slate roof. Light glowed from its sash windows and the uniformed Gatekeeper stood to greet and direct each wedding guest as they rolled through the gates.

After receiving my instructions, I continued down the driveway until the woodlands gave way to pastureland. Either side of the track, cows and sheep grazed in the fields and, in the distance, Heskitt Hall loomed, the light spilling from its rooms illuminating the twilight.

Heskitt Hall was an imposing building with an Elizabethan façade. Extended over the centuries, the original house had been built in the years following the bubonic plague that had decimated the local population. Arriving from Asia in 1348, The Black Death had swept across England the following year and wiped out more than half of the local population. The Heskitts, already powerful in the area, didn't let a good crisis go to waste and seized the opportunity of adding the land of several unfortunate families to their own and, in two cases, asserting a right of legal guardianship over the surviving heirs. It was a history that the current heir to the estate, Lady Annabelle Heskitt, didn't promote, unlike the legendary horseman of Heskitt Hall which she used to full advantage to encourage visitors. It was a successful and lucrative endeavour which had allowed her to expand the hospitality business she ran alongside her farms, as a result the Hall now boasted a thriving tourist and wedding business.

Unlike the weddings the Hall catered for, Lady Heskitt's was to be held outside. This was an unusual choice given that we were on the verge of autumn and the nights were already pulling in and edged with cold. I pulled into one of the few remaining bays in the generous carpark and then walked with my aunts to the side of the house where a gated entrance led through to a courtyard lit by strings of fairy lights and set out with tables and chairs. At the centre, taking pride of place on a stone pedestal was a life size cast bronze statue of the Headless Horseman of Heskitt Hall, a brazen reminder of the vaunted but spurious family legend. The statue was exceptionally lifelike and animated, the horse rearing its front legs as the horseman held his sword aloft as though it were a still from a film. Surrounding the statue, and adding to the drama, were lit braziers where flames leapt; they added colour and warmth to the darkening evening.

A chill ran through me as we stepped into the courtyard and I pulled my coat a little closer. "I hope the ceremony doesn't take too long," I complained.

"It is a trifle chilly," Aunt Beatrice said, pulling her coat a little closer. "We made the right choice wearing our sables."

Each Aunt wore a fur coat and Aunt Beatrice's was of fox with a huge collar and a hemline just below her calf. The coats were decades old, but tonight they glistened in perfect condition and gave my aunts a touch of glamour. Appreciative eyes followed us as we walked through the thronged guests and I was proud to be walking alongside my beautiful aunts.

"I wish Loveday and Raif were here." Aunt Euphemia's voice was laced with sorrow. "They would have loved it."

"Raif would have wanted a tour of the house," laughed Aunt Thomasin referring to Uncle Raif's love of history.

"It would have reminded him of home. I think he felt a little sad the last time we were here."

"I did notice that he had a tear in his eye when we were being shown around the great hall. It's typically Elizabethan and the Heskitt's have kept it in pristine condition."

"I think it was the portraits that really made old memories surface. One in particular, of old Sir Thomas Heskitt and his son Edmund. I think they knew each other. He said something along those lines."

"He would have been a contemporary."

"It affects us all though, doesn't it?"

"What does?"

"The loss of loved ones over the centuries. They eventually fade to memories."

"That's heart-breaking," I said. Immortality had its drawbacks. That my aunts had been alive for centuries made them fascinating but, along with their tales of times gone past, was the heartache of loss.

"It is," agreed Aunt Thomasin, "but sometimes the memories don't fade. I remember Claude so clearly …" She paused.

"Sorry!" she said, fighting back tears. "I'm feeling a little emotional!"

"Oh, Thomasin! There now." Standing beside Aunt Thomasin, Aunt Beatrice was diminutive, but she slipped an arm around the taller woman's waist and laid a head against her shoulder. Aunt Euphemia passed her a tissue.

"I'm sorry!" she repeated as a tear rolled down her cheek. "I'm making a spectacle of myself. I think it must be the wedding and ... and the thought of loves lost. Oh, dear." Her face crumpled.

"It's an emotional time, darling sister," Aunt Beatrice said. "The hex is taking its toll on us all."

"I just wish we had a magical wand and could make it all disappear."

Aunt Euphemia laughed. "Oh, sister! If only."

"But isn't that something we could do?" I asked as a thought began to develop in my mind.

"Wave a magic wand?"

"Yes. Well, I don't know ... you know ... Isn't there a way to make all of our problems disappear? Can't we create a spell, a magic wand if you like, that targets the black witch?"

"No, no, darling. Magic wands are for the television and cinema. At least, if they are used by other witches, then ... well, it's not something I've heard of."

"Magic wands?"

Silence descended among us in an instant as we exchanged glances and turned in unison to the voice. Dr. Cotta's eyes were piercing as they met mine. After our confrontation at his house over the witch-finding device, he was the very last person I wanted to see. My fingertips fizzed horribly. Instantly anxious,

I could only stare at him open mouthed, scrambling for an answer that wouldn't confirm his suspicions. How long had he been standing there? How much of our conversation had he heard? Aunt Loveday's voice rang in my memory. 'We must be careful, Livitha, with the choice of our words.' Silence descended upon our group in an instant. We had all broken our most precious rule—not to speak publicly of our powers!

"Good evening, ladies." His smile was amused. Dressed in a dark suit and white shirt that accentuated his bronzed face and white teeth, his alluring blue eyes and charismatic smile were undiminished. To add to his charm, the cologne he wore was delicious. "However, he was now someone to be feared. "Beautiful night for a wedding."

"It is," I managed. What had he heard? He could have listened in on the entire conversation! If so, last night's efforts at denying that we were witches would be seen for what they were—lies! He held my gaze. I held his longer than was comfortable, desperate to find something to say and appear unflustered and normal!

Three things happened next. I noticed Garrett watching me from across the courtyard, Mrs. Driscoll's friend Lina waved to me, and a gong rang.

Instantly flustered, and my attention caught by the two people I really wanted to talk to, I failed to answer Dr. Cotta. The crowd began to shift, and I lost sight of Garrett and then Lina.

"Are they calling us for dinner?" Aunt Beatrice asked.

"I think they want to gather us for the ceremony." Dr. Cotta gestured to a man in formal dress beckoning the guests with a gloved hand. The white fabric gleamed in the twilight. The guests were moving towards him and disappearing through an arched doorway.

Unbelievably, Dr. Cotta offered me his elbow. Not wanting to be rude, or reject him in public, I slipped my arm through his.

"Ladies," he said, addressing my aunts. "Shall we?"

Three pairs of glittering eyes watched him. Invisible to those without the gift, excited energy danced in waves around my aunts. They were conflicted. Despite their prejudice against Dr. Cotta his handsome features and gentlemanly demeanour were winning them over. He offered his other elbow. They advanced as a pack, but it was Aunt Beatrice who hooked her arm through his.

"Do you think there will be dancing?" she asked as we stepped toward the beckoning steward.

Chapter Twenty

The arched doorway opened out to a large garden. Immediately to the rear of the building was a gravelled area flanked by trees. We were led through the trees and then down a pathway lit by hanging lanterns, along the banks of a narrow lake, and then into the walled garden. Thousands of fairy lights twinkled in the growing dusk marking out a path to the wedding area. The garden was gorgeous. Formally and precisely clipped, box hedging formed an intricate pattern of beds with walkways between them. Carefully shaped and perfectly trimmed topiary of standard globes, and barley twist columns, gave height. The beds were past their best, but white roses climbed arbours dotted about the garden and shone bright in the twilight. A main walkway, lit on either side by hundreds of candles in small hurricane lamps, led to a raised area at the far end of the oblong garden where a large arch had been erected and decorated with flowers. Pinpoints of light illuminated the arch, and posts, hung with fairy lights, circled the raised area. With stars twinkling in a clear and increasingly dark sky, the scene was set.

"It's beautiful," said Aunt Thomasin.

"Just lovely," agreed Aunt Euphemia.

Without seating, the stewards organised us to stand between the beds. I didn't mind; with the night becoming increasingly chilly standing was the better option. The groom arrived with a cluster of men and passed us in a cloud of cologne. I guessed that Tarquin was in his late fifties, so similar in age to Lady Heskitt. Despite being a little on the heavy side with a growing paunch, he was attractive. A dark tan, possibly from a bottle, but maybe from weeks spent in hotter climes, made the white of his teeth pop. His grin was broad, though fixed to the point of grimace as he strode with his stag men down the walkway. With his immaculately trimmed beard, and thinning, blow-dried hair sprayed into place, he was a little too pampered for my liking.

We didn't have to wait long and several minutes after all the guests had been settled on either side of the walkway, the bride arrived. Two men dressed in eighteenth century style livery walked before the bride, each carrying a carriage lamp at the end of a pole. Behind her were another two. An elderly man with huge moustache and white lambchop whiskers, dressed in full military regalia, walked her down the aisle.

From the distance came the sound of pounding hooves.

The groom ascended the steps followed by his men.

Delicate music from a trio of classical guitarists, began to play.

A gasp ran through the guests as the bride took slow steps down the walkway, her face hidden by a short veil. The dress was a traditional style of fitted bodice and full skirt. A dazzling array of diamonds hung around her throat. They shone and glittered, lit by a rising moon. Aunt Beatrice dug an elbow in my side and whispered, the *Heskitt Inheritance*!"

"So beautiful," a guest whispered.

"Gorgeous!"

"Just divine!"

Lady Annabelle Heskitt may be over fifty years old but, in that moment, she was the most beautiful woman in the world. All eyes watched her as she made slow progress down the path.

The sound of pounding hooves grew louder.

Finally, Lady Heskitt joined her beau at the base of the steps. He took her hand to a collective 'Aah!'.

A horse whinnied.

Several guests turned to the noise.

"Is that a horse?" I asked, now aware of the pounding hooves.

The registrar stepped beneath the rose bedecked archway as Lady Heskitt and her fiancé began to ascend the steps.

The noise of galloping hooves became intrusive, and heads began to turn away from the couple.

The source of the noise became obvious within seconds. Galloping down the bridal aisle was an enormous horse complete with caped rider.

A woman screamed.

As he came into view Lady Heskitt turned from the registrar to the noise.

"It's the Headless Horseman!" I gasped as I watched the rider advance.

In the cool air, steaming breath billowed from the horse's flared nostrils and chaos erupted as the horse and its rider bore down on the guests that had clustered in the aisle. Some men were gallant and pulled their women aside. One man picked up his wife and carried her out of harm's way. A young man who stumbled was helped to stand. Others, terrified by the scene, pushed their way to safety and then stood to watch as the drama unfolded.

The horse glistened with sweat, rearing up at the jumble of people.

The headless rider, determined in reaching the podium, kicked the horse's flanks, pushing it onward.

Within seconds the horse mounted the steps and blocked Lady Heskitt and her fiancé from view. Rearing, so horse and rider resembled the bronze statue at the centre of the courtyard exactly, it then slammed its hooves down. From behind the horse, Lady Heskitt screamed. The commotion surrounding me continued although many guests watched, open-mouthed; dumb with surprise and bewildered by the terrifying wedding crasher.

Loud shouting followed and then the horseman swung down from the saddle. Tarquin's face, set to horrified shock, appeared for a moment and then he was hauled in one rough, but immensely powerful, manoeuvre to lie over the saddle where he dangled like a ragdoll.

"Oh my God!"

The crowd grew silent as the horseman tugged at the reins and the horse clattered down the steps then galloped back down the aisle and disappeared into the darkening night.

Reaction erupted.

"What just happened?"

"Has he been kidnapped?"

"That was not real!"

"Someone call the police!"

"Get an exorcist!"

"Trust her!"

All around me was confusion. More guests ran from the scene whilst others stood transfixed, curiosity replacing confusion as they stood as though watching a scene from a film. Others were cynical. Another laughed.

"I can't believe she's done this."

"Is it even a real wedding?"

"Clever stunt. I heard the Hall was having a spot of financial trouble. This is a clever way of getting some attention."

As the confused chatter continued, I considered Lady Heskitt. She stood as a statue at the top of the steps, her veil now hanging from the side of her head. Her bouquet, trampled by the horse, lay crushed on the steps. A man began a slow and sardonic clap. His partner shushed him.

"Bravo!" the cynical man shouted. "Well done. Great show."

"Oh, shut up, Barry!" his companion scolded.

"What? It's just a stunt."

"Well ... maybe it is-"

"What else can it be?"

"The Heskitt Horseman is just a myth—something to get the tourists in."

"Do you think it was just some elaborate stunt?"

"I think it's a jolly poor show! Getting us here under false pretences. We've been duped!"

"Surely not! Annabelle wouldn't be so crass!"

"Heskitt Hall is everything to her. She's always thinking of ways to make a profit and there are whispers that it's not doing so well."

"Well, that is shocking! It can't even be a real wedding!"

As I listened, I watched Lady Heskitt. If the whole thing was a stunt, then she was doing a brilliant job of playing the part of distraught bride.

"She's going to faint!" I said as Lady Heskitt began to sway.

Dr. Cotta leapt forward, running across the garden and up the steps, catching her just as her legs gave way.

Several guests, who I presumed were her real friends, had gone to Lady Heskitt's aid, but the remainder continued to chatter around me.

"Someone should call the police!"

"What good are the police against a headless horseman?"

"Hah!" the man spat with derision. "What? So you think a real headless horseman just fulfilled the Heskitt curse and stole her bridegroom?"

"Well-"

"Don't be ridiculous, Sarah. It's just a publicity stunt. See!" he said pointing to the wedding photographer who was still taking photographs. "He was taking photographs the entire time. They'll be posted on social media within ten minutes! And I'll bet you ten quid that they're on her website tomorrow and splashed all over the newspapers too."

"You're such a cynic!" she chided.

He scoffed. "So, I'm supposed to think it's real? That there really is a headless horseman?"

As they talked Dr. Cotta tended to Lady Heskitt, helped her to sit, and took her pulse. A group of guests had gathered around. Others were drifting away, confused, unsure whether to leave, or make their way to the hall where the reception was to be held.

Beside me, Aunt Thomasin hissed. "Her necklace has gone!"

Aunt Beatrice dug her elbow into my waist. "Follow him, Livitha!"

Chapter Twenty-One

"That's insane! I can't follow a horseman and definitely not a headless one!"

"Just do it! And do it quick. Here!" Aunt Beatrice fumbled in her handbag, a vintage item in glossy green shagreen, and pulled out a folded stick. "Use this!" She thrust the stick into my hands. "It extends. Unfold it. You'll find it's perfectly adequate."

"You're joking. You want me to fly – I glanced around – on a walking stick?"

"You've flown on a plastic broom and a yard broom! This is no different. Now, get going." She flicked her hand. "Follow them! Or the man will be lost forever. If the horseman takes him underground, that's the end!"

I took the folded stick as though it were contraband.

"Behind the bush," she whispered. "And take off to the right. No one will see."

"But-"

"Go!"

There was no point arguing. A quick scan of the area confirmed that all the guests were focused on the drama surrounding Lady Heskitt or were making their way to the dining room to calm themselves with another glass of free champagne. I took quick steps to a large topiary and unfolded the stick. At full length it measured about three feet long. I straddled the stick, glad that I had worn opaque tights as my wrap around dress fell either side of my legs, and I willed it to take off. To my surprise it responded instantly, and I began to feel the force of its will to rise. Several minutes had passed since the horseman had stolen the groom which meant that to have any chance of finding him, I had to fly high to get a birds-eye view.

Urging it upwards, my mind trained on a forward movement, I began to rise. "Too slow!" I hissed. "Faster!" I shot forward as though I had floored the accelerator of a powerful car, but with my hands magically locked around the stick I held steady and allowed it to power me upward. I shot from the garden like a rocket, leaving the wedding, the guests, and my aunts, behind. Veering to the right as instructed, I flew over thickening woodland. Cold brushed against my cheeks as we hurtled into the dark sky. A bird squawked, flapped its wings, and tumbled as it hit my turbulence. I scanned the area for any sign of movement, but dark had thickened and, although the moon was bright, I couldn't locate the horseman below.

Focus, Livitha! Focus.
Feel his energy.
"I'm not a bat!" I quipped. "I don't have echo location!"
Focus! the voice insisted. *Follow his energy.*

As with Aunt Beatrice, the voices were insistent and there was little point in arguing my point. I focused. At first, I could discern nothing, but as I trained my thoughts on the horseman, I felt his energy. It was strangely devoid of feeling. All I experienced was a knowledge of where his form was. I turned as I felt him turn and, after several minutes of connection, spotted him below as he galloped into a clearing.

"Got you!" I was triumphant. I had found the horseman! He galloped across the clearing and then into the woodlands where the canopy was thinner then out onto a narrow road overhung by trees.

Although the light was failing, following the horseman using my senses was easy, and I continued flying through the night sky on Aunt Beatrice's stick. This was my third experience of flight and, just as with the third, it was joyous. I rose higher, banked to the right, hovered, then swooped back down enjoying the thrill of cold air rushing through my hair. I zoned in once more onto the horseman, followed him for several moments longer, then pulled the stick back, willing it to move upwards. Defying all laws of gravity, I ascended in a spiral, unable to hold back my joy and began to giggle although it sounded far more like a cackle than was seemly! Swooping low, I caught sight of the horseman. He was slowing. I descended to the woodland canopy. As the horseman stopped, the horse's steaming breath billowed in the cold night, and a blast of freezing air buffeted me. I righted myself as the horse pawed the ground then watched as the horseman gave its flanks a sharp kick. Impossibly, it began to descend into a mound of fern-covered earth.

Pain shot through my head!

Unnoticed something had hit me from the right although in that moment I was unable discern where the pain originated. It filled my skull, the thud blotting out all thought. Disorientated, my vision blackened for crucial seconds and I felt myself being pulled upwards, out of the woodland and back above the canopy. It was a force I had never experienced before, as though I were being lifted by clamp-like hands, but I couldn't tell where they were pinching my body. Something held me in its grip, and I felt its touch everywhere.

Cold wind rushed my face as I was hurtled skyward. Seconds passed and I began to recover my senses. I was being pushed ever higher. My ears began to hurt with a sharp pain as the pressure around me changed. Thankfully, my now painfully cold hands remained magically bound to the stick. Head throbbing, the chill wind biting, I attempted to take control by forcing the stick to the right. I shot in that direction but only in an upward trajectory. I tried again, this time lowering the stick. Resistance against my efforts disappeared and I hurtled groundward, the air deafening me as I lost control and began an unhindered, earthbound, spiral. As the treetops loomed, I scrabbled through the pain in my head and my loss of orientation, to focus on slowing my fall. The voices were absent, or I was deaf to them. At any second I would crash through the canopy at top speed, magical stick or not. Smashing into earth seemed unavoidable. The stick, and my hands, grazed the top branches of a tree and then I stopped, held in the air by an invisible force, face downwards, as though frozen in time.

For several seconds I hung in the air. Fifty feet below me was the forest floor. The sense of being held had disappeared and my own magick cupped me in its hands, helping me to float just above the canopy. Heart hammering, unsure of quite what had happened, I slowly rose. I had been attacked but I had no idea by what. Unlike the grotesque imp that had fought me in the Black Woods, this foe had been invisible and now I was alone and had no idea where I was. The woods below were unfamiliar, just a vast canopy of trees, and there was no sign of the headless horseman. An effort to zone in on his energy returned a blank and I realised with shock that I was nowhere near where I had been.

I hovered for several more seconds then began tentative efforts to fly, wary of the force that had enveloped me with its pinch and thrown me thousands of feet into the sky. I shivered as cold seeped through to my bones. On the horizon, below a bright moon, snow-capped mountains shone bright in the far distance.

Snow-capped mountains!

There were no snow-capped mountains anywhere near Haligern. I began to shake. What had happened in those moments I had blacked out? Where had the force thrown me? I had been thrown upwards, the pressure in my ears and the frosty bite of the air proved that, but had I been carried across the land too?

Panic set in and I did a three hundred and sixty degree turn in a desperate effort to get my bearings. I was lost in some far-flung wilderness. Was I even still in England? Did we have mountains in England? I searched my geographical knowledge. There were mountainous hills in the Pennines, a spine that ran down the centre of the island, and there were mountain ranges in Wales and Scotland. That was all I knew. With no idea of where I was, and no idea how to navigate home, I hovered and began to think of Haligern. Moments passed as the cottage grew large in my mind, but more than just picture it, I could feel its presence. It was far in the distance. I let my senses guide me. Incredibly, I could sense my aunts and uncle too, five auras, their energy pulsing, my magical homing beacon.

I flew until the sun began to rise. Exhausted, I descended to an empty road to read a road sign. There were at least fifty more miles to travel before I came close to Haligern. I was beyond tired and the darkness which hid my peculiar mode of flight was thinning to grey. I had to get home before anyone saw me. With huge effort, I ascended to a low level and continued towards Haligern. As grey replaced black, I rose to ride just above the canopy of the Black Woods. Haligern was in the far distance, unseen, but my energy levels were critical. Flying, though thrilling, took enormous energy and, as I travelled over the woods, my energy sapped to nothing. There was no way I could make it home. With my last ounce of energy, I descended to ten feet above the ground, then, surrounded by trees, with Blackwood Manor nestled in gothic splendour about one hundred feet away, I collapsed to the ground.

As I blacked out, a pair of amber eyes watched from between the trees.

Chapter Twenty-Two

Coming round I was filled with horror. I felt its energy first, a hulking dark presence by my side. With eyes shut, I began to tremble as I listened to it breath. If it were the same creature that had fought the imp the last time I was in the Black Woods, it was a truly terrifying beast. At over six foot tall, muscular with broad shoulders, it stood on two legs, its face and body covered in dark hair, huge hands ending in long talons. If it were the same creature, I had no chance of survival. Too weak to summon any magick, and paralysed by fear, I lay still. Playing dead was my only option.

My heart hammered in my chest and I forced down a squeal of terror as I felt its breath on my cheek. This was the moment! It would take an enormous bite and rip me to shreds. A terrified mewl escaped my throat and despite my terror I opened my eyes. A pair of huge amber eyes stared down into mine. A surge of fear that began in the pit of my stomach trembled from my lips and the beast cocked its head as though listening to the sound. I snapped my eyes shut. I had lost my cover. It knew I wasn't dead. That I was not carrion. Not roadkill too rotten to eat. I was living flesh with a heart still pumping. Fresh and tasty blood. In that moment, I wished my heart would burst and send me into cardiac failure. At least then I wouldn't have to suffer the horror of being eaten alive!

A huge arm pushed beneath my shoulders, another beneath my thighs, and I felt myself being lifted. Too terrified to struggle, strong arms locked me to the beast's chest, and, with a grunt of effort, it took slow steps forward.

Metal clanked and I opened my eyes to Blackwood Manor, its turrets rising from the early morning mist in true gothic romance style.

I realised then that the creature was carrying me to the house. Held against its chest, I studied it. It was huge, with muscular pectorals and well defined abdominal muscles beneath a thick layer of soft hair that covered its torso and shoulders. Its head, like its body was covered in hair but where sharp canines protruded onto its lower lip, its nose, though distorted was more human than wolf-like. From my position, I couldn't see its eyes, but did notice long and curling lashes! It was typical. Men always seemed to have the best lashes! Men? Was it a man? *Werwulf!* Still in a state of confusion, my head began to swim as, with me cradled in its huge arms, it climbed the steps to the gothic mansion then hammered on the door. Several seconds passed. It grew impatient, and a low growl was followed by a kick at the door. Seconds later it swung open, but as I heard a man's voice, the dizziness became intense, and I passed out.

This time I came round to confusion and a crackling fire. Laid on a large velvet sofa I had been covered with a blanket. Tobias Blackwood sat in an armchair beside the fire, a book open on his knee. My head throbbed and my throat was dry. Every muscle in my body ached and, as I made an effort to sit, I groaned.

"Now, Miss Erickson, just you lie still. You've had quite an ordeal from what I can gather."

I made another effort to sit then lay back, already breathless. I had barely any energy. Outside the fog-hazed sun shone.

"What time is it?" I managed.

Tobias took a pocket watch from his waistcoat pocket. "Half past eleven."

"Half past eleven!" I tried once again to sit, but the pain in my head throbbed and I lay back down.

"Let me help you."

Minutes later, propped with cushions, blanket covering my knees, I sat with a cup of tea and a Garibaldi biscuit. Tobias looked on with bemused curiosity, the cut where Arthur had hit him still mending and surrounded by a fading bruise. Arthur's theft from Haligern cottage had taken us all by surprise, but surprise had quickly transformed to horror as we realised someone was using its power to summon creatures from the other realm. That someone had been Garrett's uncle Tobias. I had managed to stop him just at the moment the creatures were breaking through the membrane that separated our world from theirs by lobbing Arthur at Tobias. I had hit my mark and Uncle Tobias had fallen onto the steps. Nothing had been admitted, but Garrett had assured us that his uncle's efforts wouldn't be repeated. What his purpose had been remained a mystery, as did the room in the turret with the iron shackles on its fourposter bed and huge and heavy chair.

"I'm sorry about your head," I offered. When Tobias had fallen under Arthur's impact, I had been jubilant, but that joy had quickly diminished when he had cracked his head on the stone step. Regret had then turned to mortification under Garrett's accusing eyes. Today was the first time I had seen Tobias since the incident and my first opportunity to apologise.

"No need for apologies," he said, touching the damaged area on his forehead. "It's mending nicely."

"I didn't mean to hurt you."

"I understand. I'm glad that you did," he said, eyes down and fingering the book on his knee. "I was out of control. Consumed by the need to-"

The door opening halted his words and my cheeks flushed in an instant as Garrett walked in.

In that moment I wanted to shrivel beneath the blanket and disappear. I was an accidental visitor to his ancestral home once again. However, instead of an annoyed frown, he smiled, asked me if I was warm enough, helped himself to a biscuit and sat back in the armchair opposite his uncle.

I had no idea what to say. My memory was a little blurry, and my head was throbbing, but I recalled every detail of the beast that had found me in the woods and carried me up the steps. I wanted to ask a million questions, but instead took a sip of tea and bit into another Garibaldi biscuit.

"These are my favourite," I said as I took another bite, instantly regretting it as crumbs flew from my mouth. My cheeks burned. I was a bumbling wreck.

Garrett's face became serious, and, for a moment, I expected him to chide me on my manners. Instead, he said, "Liv, where were you last night?"

Flying on a folding walking cane following a headless horseman into the countryside. "Well, I went to Lady Heskitt's wedding."

He nodded. "And you disappeared from the wedding too. I know that you didn't accompany your aunts home because when you didn't return, I had to drive them back to the cottage."

"Oh, well ..." I had no idea what to say. I didn't want to lie.

"What I found odd," he continued, "was that they didn't seem particularly concerned that you had just disappeared. It bothered me immensely."

"Oh?"

"I was worried sick, that is until your Aunt Beatrice told me not to worry, that you were a big girl now, and entitled to have a social life."

My cheeks flushed. He was accusing me of going home with another man!

"Well!" I said suddenly defensive. "I can have a social life! I can see whoever I want to see."

He moved back in his chair as his face dropped.

"But I wasn't!" I blurted realising my rudeness.

"You should give me some credit, Liv. I know you're not like that and Cotta was still at the wedding until late tending to Lady Heskitt."

But I don't like Cotta! Not that way!

"Your aunts refused a lift home from him. In fact, they were quite terse with him. I guess you two have fallen out."

He looked at me from under his brows.

I nodded.

"So, are you going to tell me what's going on?"

"There's nothing going on."

He sighed. "Fine. I'll tell *you* what's going on. At least my thoughts on it. As usual, unable to resist, you took it upon yourself to follow the horseman." He waited for my response. "Am I right?"

I nodded.

"And you thought he was here? That somehow we were mixed up in this?"

"No! That's not it at all."

"Then why on earth did we find ... did you end up here, at first light ... unconscious on the doorstep? Uncle Tobias called me as soon as you were comfortable."

I was being unfair. I didn't know enough about Garrett's life, professional or personal, but he was aware of the other world, the magical, supernatural world that was unseen, even vampires and vampire hunters didn't faze him.

"It was Aunt Bea's fault," I explained. "She told me to follow him."

"I don't think blaming your aunt is fair, Liv. You're a grown woman, capable of making up your own mind."

His words irked me, but it was true. Aunt Beatrice had really only encouraged, or gave me the courage, to do what I had really wanted to do.

"Liv, we haven't been able to find Tarquin. If you have any knowledge of his whereabouts ..."

My head throbbed and since being knocked by whatever entity had attacked me as I followed the horseman, my memory was unclear. "I remember following him. He was riding through the woods, galloping along a lane and then he came out into a clearing. After that, it all goes foggy."

"And you were above the canopy?"

I had outed myself! "No!"

"Liv ..."

Uncle Tobias chuckled.

"I know the truth. I know about the coven. Haligern history is not a secret to the Blackwoods, just as I know our history is known to your family." He leant forward. "We're cut from the same cloth, you and I."

"You're among friends here," Uncle Tobias coaxed.

"Then yes, I was above the canopy ..."

"On a broom?"

"A stick," I admitted.

"A stick? Impressive." Uncle Tobias chuckled and his eyes gleamed behind his gold-rimmed spectacles.

"That must have been quite a sight."

"Oh, I kept low so that no one saw me."

The two men burst into friendly laughter, but Garrett quickly grew serious. "Liv. I think you may be the only one who can help with this bizarre case. We've searched all night with no leads. Will you help us?"

"Me? Help you?"

He smiled. "Yes, you seem to have an instinct for these things and since I lost my sidekick to Vlad the Impaler, I need another partner."

I was taken aback, terrified, and thrilled all in the same moment. "But ... I have to run the shop!"

"I'm not asking you to change your job, just help me on this case. It's an unusual one and my boss isn't taking it seriously."

"Oh! But he must. The horseman is real!"

"You and I know that, but they don't, and I can't enlighten them. They think it's all a prank and suspect Lady Heskitt is involved."

"To gain attention for the Hall?"

"Yep. It doesn't help that someone uploaded a video to social media that's gone viral. It's certainly not going to hurt business."

"Notoriety has its own rewards," chipped in Uncle Tobias.

Despite aching with exhaustion, I agreed.

"Great! Finish your tea. I'll take you home."

Chapter Twenty-Three

We arrived at Haligern just after midday. The mist had lifted, and the sun shone with a brilliance and warmth that gave the house and its early autumn gardens, a haze of country cottage glamour.

"It's certainly beautiful."

"I love it!" My heart filled with warmth. Being with Garrett at Haligern, so close to the only other people in the world I truly loved, was joyous. My belly did a flip. I was with Garrett outside Haligern, and my aunts were inside! What would they think? I had disappeared, hadn't called, and was now rolling up in last night's clothes with a man from a family they professed to detest. Could a walk of shame be any more dreadful? *Of course they won't think that of you! Calm down. You followed the horseman and were attacked. They'll understand. Now buck up and get inside!*

"Liv? Are you alright?" Garrett had noticed the change. I had flipped from joy to mortified despair and anxiety within seconds. Could he read my mind? Or my aura? Or feel my energy? How deep did his own magick run?

"Sure, why?"

"Well, your smile instantly disappeared and now you look like someone just died."

I had given myself away! I couldn't lay the whole neurotic mess that was Liv Carlton née Erickson's newly separated, menopausal, hormonally challenged self on Garrett but I decided to share what was really causing me stress. "It's just ... there's so much going on. My aunt and uncle are really sick, Haligern's practically falling down-"

"Your aunt is sick?"

"Yes, and the house ... She's being poisoned. Just come in and you'll see." Showing Garrett how Haligern and my aunt were being poisoned was easier than explaining it all.

"Perhaps I should wait here. I'm not exactly flavour of the month right now."

"That's true, but I want you to come inside. And my aunts may be able to help with the case. And I want you to see what's happening to Haligern." I had already decided to ask for his help. As a Detective Chief Inspector, he had a special set of skills we could use.

Climbing the steps, a shard of stone broke free from the edge and I noticed that the rose arch that framed the door had begun to rot and the roses wither. Worse, the front door opened to an odour of mildew and the hinges creaked. A large crack had appeared in the wall behind the hallway mirror and on the console table, the roses cut by Mrs. Driscoll yesterday to 'cheer' us all up, were pitted with mould.

Garret's reaction, a disbelieving gasp, made the pit of my stomach roil. I had seen the devastation, but Garrett confirmed my fears. Haligern was in a rapid decline, crumbling and decaying at an accelerated rate. Only a few steps in, I paused, repulsed. If the house had decayed this much overnight, what state would my aunt and uncle be in? Images of ancient faces with liver-spotted, paper-thin skin, wrinkled and sagging with eyes faded by time, swam in my imagination.

"Liv?" Garrett took my arm.

"It's worse than I thought! We cast a charm to counter the hex. Aunt Loveday was feeling better ... but this is worse!" My voice was hoarse as I held back my emotion.

Garrett slipped a comforting arm over my shoulder. "We'll sort it, Liv. Everything will be alright."

I had no idea if he could really help, but in that moment his words were all I wanted to hear. I sniffed back tears and nodded. He gave my shoulder a tight squeeze. Voices drifted from the kitchen. "Come on, let's talk to your aunts. See if there's anything the Blackwoods can do. The horseman and the Heskitts will have to wait."

His kindness was the last straw and tears spilled over my lashes. "Give me a second."

"Take a step away from the emotion, Liv," he whispered. "A good detective is objective. Keeping a clear head and a cold heart is the best way to help your aunt and uncle right now."

I nodded. He was right. I had to stay calm and in control of my emotions. A pathetic blubbering wreck was no help to anyone. His words worked like magic to stem the flow of tears and I wiped them away with the tissue he offered. "Come on," I said with a grim smile. "Let's go in."

My fears were, to some extent, unfounded. I had dreaded walking in and seeing Aunt Loveday or Uncle Raif in an advanced stage of ageing. However, although there was evidence of increased deterioration in the kitchen, neither Aunt Loveday nor Uncle Raif were present and my other aunts' appearance was unchanged.

"Liv!" Aunt Beatrice's relieved smiled only flickered a fraction as her eyes flitted from me to Garrett. "Thank goodness you're back," she said with an obvious effort not to react to Garrett's presence. "We were worried."

"Tell us! What happened? Did you discover where the horseman went?"

"Did you find Tarquin?"

Bombarded with questions I remained silent. The horseman and Lady Heskitt's troubles were now at the back of my mind.

"The step broke."

"The step?"

"Yes, it broke when I came in, and the hallway ... everything is rotting! What happened to the protective spell we cast?"

Aunt Thomasin's reserve broke. "It didn't work!"

"But it was working! Aunt Loveday was getting better."

"We think whoever is poisoning us ..." Aunt Thomasin pursed her lips together. "I'm not sure we should be talking about this ... in front of a Blackwood."

Aunts Beatrice and Euphemia exchanged worried glances. The atmosphere was suddenly tense.

"Garrett is one of us. Plus, he's a detective," I said in his defence. "He may be able to help."

"Hmm."

"It's highly unorthodox ..."

"Banishment excludes them from the covens."

Garrett sighed heavily. "I'm here to help, ladies, but only if you want my help."

Aunt Thomasin glared, then softened her expression. "Sisters, I think that we must put our prejudice aside, for the sake of Loveday and Raif." She gave each of the aunts a meaningful look and all three turned their backs as they huddled to discuss the situation. Aunt Thomasin raised her arm, flicked her hand, and a haze of shimmering, iridescent light enveloped them, and the room grew silent.

"A shield of privacy," Garrett said.

"You know what it is?"

"I've heard of them, but never seen it. Uncle Tobias talks a lot about his youth."

I was about to ask him questions when Lucifer appeared at my feet. Startled, I yelped in surprise. Lucifer's vampire-like canines shone bright against his dark fur as he smirked. "Don't do that, Lucifer," I chided with disapproval. Startling me was his newest thing! And each time he caught me out his smirk grew more satisfied. I never saw the funny side of being startled.

He withheld a chuckle. "I've been waiting for you to return from your ... galivanting!"

"I have not been galivanting!"

"Well, what do you call it when you roll up at midday still dressed in your evening wear from the night before, hair messed up, makeup smeared? Why, you look nothing more than a cheap harlot this morning, Livitha!"

Garrett snorted as he held back a laugh.

"Now just hold on, Lucifer!" Despite my innocence, my cheeks burned. Did I really look that bad?

"I have not had any breakfast," he complained.

"Well ... It was impossible for me to get back home before now."

"That's not an excuse to starve a man to death!" he sniffed.

I bit back my retort that he wasn't actually a man. "Well …" I noticed his newly washed bowl on the drainer. "Are you sure that you haven't had breakfast, Lou?"

"… Yes!"

"Then why is your bowl on the drainer?" His bowl was always washed and put away after each meal—Aunt Beatrice was particularly particular about it.

"Well … I could have starved."

"Really?"

"Yes! Really. It was only the kindness of your aunts that saved me from savage hunger."

I resisted the urge to tell him he could catch his own breakfast. He was a capable hunter and often relished a mouse or a bird – much to my chagrin – before breakfast.

"Liv!"

"Yes, Lou!"

"Liv, I'm thirsty."

"Right. Well, I can get you some water."

He shook his head.

"Milk?"

"Pah!"

I groaned inwardly. He wasn't going to stop nagging until I caved in and I was in no mood to challenge him. "Port?"

His fang grew in prominence. "That would suffice."

I took Lucifer's saucer from the drainer and reached for the port.

"You're kidding!" quipped Garret.

"It's only a little."

"Yes, but port?"

Lucifer glared at Garret. "Don't interfere!"

Garrett raised his palms in mock surrender.

"Fatuous man!"

"Lou," I said in stern tones. "Behave yourself." I placed the saucer on the floor and poured out a small taste of port. Lucifer rubbed up against my leg and began to purr. "And he's not really a cat you know."

Lucifer dropped his head to lick at the port.

"Wow! That is one sour puss," Garrett quipped.

Lucifer eyed him with disdain before returning his attention to the saucer.

"Oh, he's just grumpy because I wasn't here to give him breakfast. Isn't that right little kitty," I cooed this loudly. Lucifer hated me calling him kitty.

With this, he swished his tail, lapped at the port, then turned on me. "Yes, Winifred, that is correct."

"Why you!"

"It is improper for a witch to return at midday having neglected her familiar! I only hope that your declining reputation doesn't sully mine."

I glowered at him. "Well, I-"

"No!" He held up a paw. "Don't apologise."

"I wasn't going-"

"I'm far too wounded to consider an apology—at the moment."

"Lucifer!"

"I will expect full reparations, obviously." He stared at me with green eyes sparkling, his fangs revealed as he smirked. "Now, as they say in these times ... later!" With that he jumped across the floor towards the hearth and disappeared.

"I see you've got him well under control, Liv," laughed Garrett. "I thought familiars were meant to be a witch's servant."

"Well, he's more of a companion. Sometimes he's lovely. Honest. I think the stress of everything is getting to him too."

The iridescent glaze of Aunt Thomasin's privacy shield disappeared, and all three aunts turned to face us.

Chapter Twenty-Four

"We have decided that this emergency overrides Council rule," Aunt Thomasin explained. "So ... DCI Blackwood-"

"Please, call me Garrett."

"So, Garrett, if you would like to join us in our efforts to find the criminal poisoning of our beloved sister, then we gladly accept your help."

"It would be my honour to help," Garrett answered with grace.

"Then let us sit. We must put our collective knowledge together and discover a way forward. The culprit must be stopped, or all will be lost."

Murmurs of agreement filled the room.

"I'll put the kettle on," Aunt Beatrice said with decision. "Tea always helps."

Garrett joined us at the kitchen table whilst Aunt Beatrice spooned fresh leaves into the teapot and covered them with hot water from the kettle.

Minutes later we were all seated, cups of tea in hand, and ready to discuss the case and all its details.

"We have a possible lead," I said as Garrett took a sip of his tea.

"That's good. Let's hear about it then."

"Well ..." I looked to my aunts for permission. They nodded in response. "We think that a witch called Hegelina Fekkitt is responsible."

"The name doesn't ring a bell."

"Your Uncle Tobias would know about her. She was exiled a long time ago, for using the death-bringing tree."

"Wasn't that outlawed in the sixteenth century?"

I was impressed. "Yes, it was!"

Garrett threw me a smile. "So, why do you think that she's the culprit?"

"We found a death-bringing gallows-"

"And a ring of poison tethers," interrupted Aunt Beatrice.

"That's right. Thank you, Beatrice. We found gallows in the woods and a connected ring of tethers around the house."

"That's why Loveday is so sick!"

"That's what we believe to be true," Aunt Euphemia agreed.

"And apart from Hegelina Fekkitt being exiled for using it and finding one on Haligern land, why do you think that she is the one attacking Loveday?" Garrett asked.

"Because Aunt Loveday was on the Council of Witches when they sentenced her to exile."

"Ah! I see."

"And she has recently been released from exile and is currently on parole."

"Although she hasn't reported in to her Parole Officer."

Garrett nodded. "I think that's a solid enough reason for suspicion. So, do we have any way of identifying Ms. Fekkit?"

"Nope!" I said. "There's a woodcut of her in one of Dr. Cotta's books, but it's not a good enough portrait to know what she looked like."

"But if Loveday sentenced her to exile, doesn't she know what she looks like?"

I shook my head. "We've tried that already, but the poison is making her thinking fuddled and she's having difficulty remembering things."

"I see.

"So, I'm not sure where to go from here. We have a suspect, but don't know where to find her."

"Actually, perhaps we do," said Aunt Thomasin.

"Oh?"

"Well, more of a lead that may help?" She shrugged her shoulders.

"And?" encouraged Garret.

"Well, we were talking last night, after the incident at Heskitt Hall-"

"Lady Anabelle's problems cannot be our priority!" I insisted.

Aunt Thomasin held my gaze and pursed her lips. "If you would let me finish, Livitha, you will understand my point."

"Sorry! Please, go on." My cheeks began to prickle.

"After Dr. Cotta had dropped us off-"

"Not before."

"No, obviously not before. Thank you, Beatrice. Once we were alone again, we were free to discuss the events and as we were reminiscing about the Heskitt's and their curse, one thing revealed itself ..."

"Which was?"

"That the Heskitts, Loveday, and Old Aggie are connected."

"Who is Old Aggie?" Garrett asked.

"You may know her as Aggie Sampson."

"Oh, yes. Uncle Tobias has told me a few tales about her."

"Well, she has been struck by the same malady as Loveday. She is ageing rapidly."

"It's true," I said. "I went to see her. She has gone from being a vibrant woman in her sixties to a frail geriatric in a matter of weeks. We think that Hegelina is attacking her too."

"But how is Lady Heskitt connected? She looked quite beautiful last night and doesn't appear to be ageing rapidly," Garrett said, "She's not even a witch. At least not to my knowledge."

"That is correct. The Heskitt's do not have magic running through their veins. They have avarice, lust, and greed, but not magick."

"So how are the three connected?"

"Well, we think that the theft of Lady Annabelle's groom is an act of revenge, against the family. It was a Heskitt who originally accused her of witchcraft, for which she was on trial. She evaded execution by using her magick to make the goalers believe that she was her cellmate and an innocent died in her place."

"Sally Empringham, a widow with young children. The Council felt compelled to take care of them as Hegelina was one of their coven members. The use of magick had effectively sentenced the young mother to death."

"She was due to be released that morning having been found not guilty of the charge for which she had been accused."

"The tragic deceit was Hegelina's first strike, but it was her use of the death-bringing tree and some outlawed magick that got her exiled."

"Ah! I see. That does make sense."

"It does!" I agreed.

"So," continued Aunt Thomasin with a smile, "the horseman may lead us to Hegelina."

Beatrice and Euphemia nodded in enthusiastic agreement.

"That's a great idea, but may I suggest something?" Garrett asked.

"Yes."

"Please, go ahead."

"Well, Liv mentioned that the house has deteriorated badly since yesterday, and you said Loveday and Raif are far frailer, so if the circle was working yesterday then it has perhaps been sabotaged?"

"Garrett could be right."

"Then we must repair it!"

"If we shore up our own magick, it could give us the time that we need to discover where exactly Hegelina is hiding."

With us all in agreement, Aunt Thomasin led us to the protective circle placed around the house yesterday. The problem was evident immediately. The twine and its attached protective tethers were no longer surrounding the cottage.

"It's gone!"

"But we placed a shield of protection around Haligern, so that no strangers could enter. How could she have broken through?"

"Maybe it's not her? Maybe she's not the one poisoning Loveday?"

"But who else?"

"Loveday has lived far too long not to have made enemies."

"As have we all."

"But Hegelina is the only one with connections to Loveday, Aggie, and Lady Heskitt."

"The only one we know of. There could be others."

"I can't think of any."

"That doesn't mean they don't exist."

"True."

We spent the next hour creating a new protective circle and reinforced it with a particularly strong protective spell that Aunt Euphemia found in her grimoire along with one Aunt Beatrice found that focused on cleansing the house of the radiating poison. "It's kind of like a disinfectant, but for magical poison," she explained.

After checking in on Loveday and Raif, we turned our attention back to the incident at Heskitt Hall.

"Tell us what happened when you followed the horseman, Liv."

I readily agreed. "Well, I caught up with him as he rode out of the entrance gates of Heskitt Hall and then ..." It was then that I realised I had no memory of following the horseman. I remembered everything that had happened that evening up to that point. "I can't remember!"

"Try, Liv," Garrett encouraged.

I tried again. Again, nothing. "I just can't. There's nothing!"

"It's okay. Just stay calm."

I sagged in my chair. "I'm sorry!"

"You had a knock to the head. You could be concussed. Once you've had a good sleep-"

"We don't have that long!" blurted Aunt Euphemia. "I don't think Loveday will ... will last much longer!" Her voice held a deep despair.

A chill ran through me. "I'm so sorry!" Tears began to prick my eyes.

"I can help you remember," said Aunt Beatrice.

"How?"

"Well, as you know, I can sometimes read your thoughts ..."

"You listen in, you mean."

"Yes, well, in my defence, you are rather loud, Livitha."

I sighed and raised my brows in indulgent martyrdom.

"Well, anyway, I may be able to zone in – as they say these days – and read your memories."

"Now that's a wonderful idea," enthused Aunt Euphemia. "Fabulous!"

I didn't feel particularly comfortable with the idea. "Well-"

"And whilst you're there, find out where she buried my silver brooch when she was four. I never did find it."

"Now's not the time for frippery, sisters. Next time-"

"There won't be a next time!" I blurted in horror. "This is the one and only time I will be letting anyone inside my head. Ever!" I shuddered at the thought of Aunt Beatrice having access to my most intimate memories. It would be like having my life televised in some hideous, fly-on-the-wall documentary!

"Now, don't worry darling. I won't pry."

I shuddered. She was still listening in! "Please! Can we just get on with it?"

"We can."

"Is it safe?" asked Garrett. He seemed less than enthusiastic.

"It is. Now, both of you stop fussing!" Aunt Beatrice guided me to a chair and sat facing me. Taking both hands in hers, she instructed me to close my eyes and relax.

"Is this going to hurt? Will I feel you in there?"

"Shh! Let me work. Now, Livitha, think back to the wedding and the moment the horseman arrived."

As instructed, I closed my eyes and took myself back to last night. As with all forced efforts, other memories often intrude, particularly when we don't want them to, and I was back in the courtyard at the moment I had spotted Garrett. My heart raced as our eyes met.

Aunt Beatrice squeezed my hands. "Tsk! Focus, Livitha."

Increasing my efforts, I felt myself fall deep into another level of consciousness. The noises in the kitchen faded and all I was aware of was the image playing out in my mind. Like scenes from a silent movie, they were without colour and the movement of their characters lacked a steady flow. The next face to come forward was Lina. I peered through the crowd, but just as had happened at the wedding, she disappeared. The wave of disappointed washed over me as it had last night.

Lady Heskitt walked down the aisle, diamonds glinting beneath the collar of her fur stole. Next, I heard the pounding hooves and then the horseman galloped past me. As though I were still there, the earthy sweat of the horse mingled with the sulphuric reek of the horseman. The horse reared. Lady Heskitt screamed, clutching at her neck, and then I was flying, exhilarated as I powered upwards, the sky sparkling with its trillion, glittering diamonds against a raven sky. I lost myself in the moment, revelling in the sensation of joy running through my veins. Cold hands squeezed mine and Aunt Beatrice's voice whispered 'Focus! Only focus on the horseman, Livitha! Find him.'

I was above the canopy, following the horseman. He galloped from the dense woodlands following the road that cut through the clearing and then passed to the other side. I followed the road, riding high above the horseman. Behind me lay Heskitt Hall and northbound, in the direction the horseman was headed, was St. Michael's, a medieval church known for its prominent steeple. To the west, at the point where the horseman stopped was a wind turbine. Pain wracked through my head as I remembered the attack and I jolted in the chair before falling to the floor.

"Stop this now!" Garrett's voice carried irresistible authority and Aunt Beatrice retreated from my mind.

"Well, now we know where the horseman stopped," she said with satisfaction.

Garret crouched beside me. "Liv, are you alright?" He took my hand, stroking my fingers.

I nodded although the remembered strike to my head from last night's attack was throbbing with real pain.

"Give her this." Aunt Euphemia thrust a mug at Garrett. "It has a calmative. It will help her relax."

I took a sip gladly, enjoying the sensation of calm that flowed from my stomach through to each muscle. It even softened the pain in my head.

I now remembered how I'd followed the horseman through the woods, how I had listened to the ancestral voices and focused on his energy, feeling him rather than seeing him. "I watched him disappear before I was attacked. It was as though the woods swallowed him!"

"It did."

"But that's not possible."

"If a Headless horseman kidnapped Lady Heskitt's groom, then I'm sure a tree swallowing them both is also possible."

"It looked as though he galloped into a mound of earth rather than into a particular tree," I explained.

"The tree thing is from another legend, from our American cousins."

"Ah, yes, indeed. Such a savage horseman! We're very lucky."

"Lucky?"

"Yes, dear. The other horseman, the one from the New World, well, he was a true savage, one of those people who loves to cause carnage and can be called upon to rise, but when he does, he chops off the heads of his victims."

"Well, technically, they're not *his* victims, if he has been called to rise, Euphemia."

"True. They're the victims of the caller."

"Just as Tarquin is Hegelina's victim."

"If it is her who called the horseman."

"True."

The backwards and forwards conversation was like mental ping pong and I shook my head as though to clear my thoughts. "So ... do you believe that the horseman will kill the groom?"

"We do."

"Very likely."

"He usually does."

"Usually?"

"Of course, this is not his first rodeo." Aunt Beatrice chuckled at her joke.

"Beatrice, this is not the time to make light of the situation."

"What do you mean, 'not his first rodeo'?"

"It has been such a long time since he rode," Aunt Beatrice said then closed her eyes, deep in thought. "But if I remember rightly, the last time he was called upon, which was ... now let me see ... Oh, my, at least ... more than two hundred years ago! Can you believe it sisters? Do you remember? It didn't end well. By the time they found the man he abducted, he had been dead for several days."

"Beheaded?"

"No, that's not his modus operandi."

"Well, what is his modus operandi?"

"Well, suffocation, interred alive ... in the earth."

Garrett stood, signalling the end of the conversation. "Time is running short ladies. It's time to find our horseman."

A shiver of excitement ran through me.

"If that's the case," said Aunt Thomasin. "I'm coming too."

Chapter Twenty-Five

With Aunt Thomasin insisting that she could be helpful during the investigation, Garrett agreed to her demand, and we motored into the village less than half an hour later. I was surprised at the amount of traffic. There were also a number of news vans.

"The video of the horseman abducting Tarquin went viral," Garrett explained. "It's all over social media."

As Garrett drove, I typed 'headless horseman' into my phone's browser and followed a link with Heskitt in the title. The link took me to a video of the wedding. I watched it with interest as the video showed panoramic views of the gathered guests, grimaced as I noticed myself in the crowd, smiled as I noticed Lina and then Garrett, frowned when I recognised Dr. Cotta. A running commentary accompanied the footage.

There was a slight fuzziness about the video and the lighting made it impossible to see clearly, but there was a horse, complete with headless horseman. The video zoomed in as the groom was lifted onto the horse. The videographer's hand trembled and his voice became over-excited as the horseman galloped away with his victim. He then turned his focus on Lady Heskitt. With hand splayed across the base of her throat where the diamond necklace had been, she stood with horrified disbelief stamped on her face. I scrolled through the comments. Most had decided it was a publicity stunt and that the horseman was a fake. Some of the more observant had noticed the missing jewels and were claiming it was a robbery. Only a few believed that it was a real horseman, and these were unsparingly derided by the social media trolls.

"Well, looks like the jury has decided the horseman is a fake. The only question is whether it was a publicity stunt cooked up by the Heskitt's or a robbery. She was wearing a collar full of diamonds when she walked down the aisle, but they disappeared along with the groom."

"The Heskitt Inheritance."

"I guess it was part of her inheritance."

"That's what the collar of diamonds is called. 'The Heskitt Inheritance.'"

"Oh, I see. Is that a thing then? Giving necklaces a name."

"It is, dear," answered Aunt Thomasin. "Particularly expensive items, or gems, are often given names. Take the 'Heart of the Ocean', it's worth twenty million United States dollars. I heard that the 'Heskitt Inheritance' was worth around eight million."

"Wow! That is a lot. No wonder Lady Heskitt looked so horrified."

Surprised at how knowledgeable she was, I re-watched the video and scrutinised the moment the horseman lifted the groom. His knee seemed to bend at the moment he was lifted. I couldn't tell whether he was backing away in fear or jumping to aid the horseman. "I know that we're more open to accepting that magick could be at play," I said as I pressed replay, "but do you think it's possible that the horseman is a fake?"

"Not a real headless horseman, you mean?"

"Yes. It did look impressive, but with all the advances in prosthetics and animatronics I'm not sure …"

"Well, let's look at the evidence."

"He was strong," I said. "The way he lifted the groom up and slung him over the saddle would have taken immense strength."

"Superhuman strength?"

"Or supernatural strength?"

On learning the value of the 'Heskitt Inheritance', I had become deeply suspicious of motive. "Would it be possible for the horseman to pull him up, assuming he is human, if he was given help?"

"Help? How do you mean?"

"If, for example, the groom jumped up just as the horseman grabbed him?" I asked.

"Well, I guess it's possible," agreed Garrett, "but it would have taken great timing."

"They're a horsey lot, the Heskitts," added Aunt Thomasin. "And so are the Sotheby-Joneses."

"The toffs always are," agreed Garrett and then grew silent. "Knowing how much that necklace is worth, really does change things."

"It does."

"I'm not sure we're looking at revenge here."

"I have my doubts too," I agreed. "But then, I was attacked as I hovered above him. No human could have done that."

"That's true," Aunt Thomasin agreed. "Such a conundrum!"

"Well," Garrett said taking the road that would take us past Heskitt Hall, "whichever it is, we still need to locate the place where the horseman disappeared."

We continued along the road in silence until Garrett spoke.

"To my mind," Garrett said, breaking the silence. "There are several options. One. Lady Heskitt or someone involved in the business arranged his abduction as a publicity stunt. Two. It was the headless horseman, raised by Hegelina Fekkit as an act of revenge against Lady Annabelle's ancestor. Three. Lady Heskitt has been robbed and Tarquin may be an accomplice. Four. Tarquin Sotheby-Jones has been kidnapped, in which case we can expect a demand for ransom. In three of those four scenarios, Tarquin is in mortal danger.

"And if it *is* the real horseman?"

"Then I'm afraid it could already be too late. We may find a body.

Chapter Twenty-Six

As we motored past Heskitt Hall, Garrett pulled into the side of the road, retrieved a map from the glove compartment, then folded it out over the steering wheel. He fumbled in the inner pocket of his jacket and fished out a pair of glasses.

"You wear glasses?"

"Yep, I'm no spring chicken, Liv! It comes to us all."

With the glasses on, he studied the map, peering over the lenses to look across the horizon. He reminded me of a young version of his uncle. In that moment I saw the old man he would become and knew that I wanted to be there with him when that time came.

"Right, so as far as I can tell, the place where you saw the horseman disappear into the earth is about three-quarters of a mile from here. If we follow the road towards Saxilby and stop where the turbine is adjacent, we may have a chance of finding the exact spot."

"There could be other evidence," Aunt Thomasin added.

He gave her his attention.

"Well, there could be tracks in the soil, where the horses' hooves trampled through the undergrowth."

"That's right. Finding tracks would certainly help." He offered her a smile.

Aunt Thomasin glowed in his approval.

I sensed that despite her prejudice, she was warming to him.

Three-quarters of a mile later, Garrett pulled onto the verge and we disembarked.

"Now, you said that the horseman followed this road and then disappeared into a mound of earth."

"Yes."

"On which side did he leave the road."

"That would have been ... to the right."

"Are you sure?"

"Positive."

"That's helpful. We'll focus on the right side of the road. Thomasin, could you search the verge for signs of hoof prints, please. Liv, if you could check further into the forest for sign of any structures through the trees. I'll walk behind you both and look for any signs of entry."

It was a sensible plan, and we set off walking at a reasonable pace. One tree quickly came to resemble another and after ten minutes of scrutinising the woods, I began to doubt we would find the spot where the horseman left the road. "I was sure it was here," I said, beginning to feel a little foolish. Had I got it wrong?

"We just have to be patient," Aunt Thomasin coached. "It is rather like finding a needle in a haystack though. All the ferns and grass meld into one the harder you try to see."

Another ten minutes passed, and I began to pick up a strange energy. There was nothing to see in the woods, but I could feel its shape and colour. Amorphous and black it was like a wisp of smoke but there, nevertheless. I stopped to peer through the trees. "It's this way," I said, convinced that we would find something although I couldn't be sure of what.

"Have you found tracks?" Garrett called from behind.

"I'm not sure, but I have a feeling about something." Distracted as I tramped into the woodland, I was unaware of Garrett's response. I scanned the surrounding trees, zoning in on the invisible energy and veered to the right. Twigs snapped underfoot and I picked up my pace, eventually running.

"Liv!"

Ignoring Aunt Thomasin's call, I continued running and then I saw it. A grassy hillock among the trees.

"It's here," I called.

"Okay, no need to shout." Garrett was at my side and as I took another step towards the mound, he gripped my arm. "Just hold back. Let's wait for your aunt and take a moment to check around. We may not be the only ones here."

He was right. I was rushing in.

Breathless, but with eyes glittering, Aunt Thomasin joined us. "There it is," she whispered. "This *is* exciting!"

"It is!" I agreed.

"Did you feel it's energy, Livitha?"

"I did. Can you?"

"Yes. Faint but there, something dark and a little tragic."

"I felt that, although there is anger too."

"Agreed."

"I feel nothing," Garrett said.

"That's because you're blocked, dear."

Garrett grunted and took a step towards the mound. "Let's take a look then, shall we?"

We were approaching the mound from the side so moved to the front.

"Hah!"

"What is it?"

"Doors!"

The mound was fronted by doors, set at a low angle. The entranceway to the mound.

"Could be an old bunker," Garrett said. "There are quite a few around here, old Anderson bunkers from World War II."

"But aren't they usually close to houses? We're quite a distance from any buildings. It would be a little tricky running all the way here when the sirens sounded. The bombing would be over before you got here."

Garrett scanned the trees. "It's possible there was a house here at some point, the trees are mature, but not ancient. We could be standing in what was once a garden," he suggested.

"Well," I said with impatience. "We won't know unless we look! What are we waiting for?"

"Ladies, first then." Garrett gestured to the doors with a dramatic sweep of his arm and a smile.

"Well ... I think we should do it together."

Opening the slanted doors revealed concrete steps and a definite horsey whiff rose to our nostrils. Ahead, the space was dark. Beside me, Aunt Loveday clicked her fingers, and a globe of bright and sparkling energy filled her hand. To my surprise, she stepped down first. "Come along then! Let's take a look."

With the light to brighten the space, we took tentative steps down. I counted ten, nearly as many as in a typical staircase. "It's deep!"

"And cold."

The steps led us to an oblong space with an arched roof.

"I think it *is* an old Anderson shelter," Garrett said. "I visited one a few years ago, and it was just like this."

I lit a witch ball of my own and headed to the back of the long room. It was empty but there was evidence of recent activity and black hoof marks were stamped onto the concrete floor. I stooped to retrieve a stalk of hay. "Well, its certain that a horse has been here, and they fed it too," I held up the stalk.

"So, it was a real horse," Garrett stated.

"I think so. You can smell it."

"Well, that settles one thing. We're not dealing with anything supernatural."

"I'm not so sure," said Aunt Thomasin. "I think what we're dealing with here is definitely of the supernatural kind, at least, it is beyond the natural world." She held out her hand to show a small fabric doll. It had white hair tied in an old woman's bun and wore a roughly made plaid dress. At its centre, stabbed through the dress, were a trio of long pins.

I recognised the fabric at once. "It's a poppet! Of Aunt Loveday."

Chapter Twenty-Seven

After 'de-activating' the poppet with an 'interfering' charm, Aunt Thomasin removed the pins, and placed it into her pocket.

As we left the 'bunker' we took care not to step on the hoof prints and made our way back to the road where we waited for Garrett. He took numerous photographs and then joined us with a satisfied look on his face. His eyes glinted. "It's a great start," he said.

I agreed but couldn't shift my frustration. "But we're still no closer to finding Hegelina."

"But we know, okay, not for certain, but we're pretty sure she's involved in all three crimes."

"And that she didn't call the horseman."

"Which means that she's not as powerful as we feared," confirmed Aunt Thomasin.

"And that she has an accomplice."

"Or accomplices."

We grew silent as we mulled over the puzzle. The thought of returning back to Haligern without having stopped the hex was depressing. "Shall we go for a coffee?" I suggested.

"Great idea. I'm parched."

"Why don't we go back to Heskitt Hall. They have a coffee shop, and usually some lovely cakes."

It was agreed, and we arrived at the *Headless Horseman Coffee Shop* minutes later.

Coffee ordered and cakes chosen, we sat before a huge plate glass window that overlooked the courtyard and the bronze statue of the horseman. The early autumn sun was beginning to lower on the horizon and shone with mellow brightness making the converted stables even more airy and bright.

"It is lovely here," Aunt Thomasin said, "but I have to be honest, I'm quite disappointed that the horseman turned out to be a fake!"

"Me too!" I agreed. "It kind of takes the shine off it."

"Well, I'm relieved," said Garrett. "At least now the police can do their job. These supernatural cases cause me a lot of grief!" He took a sip of coffee.

I waited for him to continue, to give an example of a supernatural case that had given him a lot of grief, but he only placed a great forkful of carrot cake into his mouth. Frosting sat on his top lip. If I'd been with Pascal I'd have coughed and given him a meaningful look, but as the frosting bobbed up and down as Garrett chewed through his cake with relish, I was mesmerised. I wanted to lean over and kiss it from his lips.

Aunt Thomasin coughed.

I cast her a glance, cheeks beginning to burn, unsure if she'd read my thoughts. She threw a sideways glance at Garrett as he continued to chew and nodded her head in a 'tell him!' gesture. I shook my head and stifled a giggle. She rolled her eyes.

"Ahem! DCI ... Garrett. If you don't mind me saying, you appear to have frosting on your lip."

"Sorry!" Taking a napkin, he wiped his lips. "All gone?"

"Yes, all gone," Aunt Thomasin confirmed.

"I was just thinking."

"Hmm?"

"Well, what's new around the village?"

I shook my head. "I don't know. It's just the same as always, really."

"Yes, apart from Old Aggie and your aunt coming under attack and a horseman abducting a groom and stealing the Heskitt Inheritance, there's nothing new!"

"Well, yes, but there's nothing else I can think of."

"What about visitors? Newcomers? Unusual activity? You said that this whole thing kicked off about three weeks ago which coincided with the release of Hegelina from exile in the other realm."

I nodded.

"And she has had access to Haligern land."

"On two occasions that we're aware of."

"She was present at the wedding."

"I don't think she was."

"Well, what I mean is that she knocked you off your broom-"

"It was a stick."

"Yes, well, she knocked you sideways, so she must have been observing the wedding."

"Yes, I guess so."

"Well, what has she done to Old Aggie? If she's a victim of Hegelina too, she must have done something. Ringed the house with poison tethers as she did at Haligern perhaps?"

"You're right. We haven't checked. It's certainly possible."

"And you think we should pay Aggie a visit?"

"I do."

I wasn't sure how going to Aggie Sampson would help. Even if we did find a ring of poison around the house it would only confirm what we already knew. But removing it may help.

Chapter Twenty-Eight

"Hsst!" The noise left my lips before I had a chance to stop it. Aggie Sampson's front door, hanging on the handle was a tether. The fabric wasn't the same as those we had found at Haligern, but the construction was identical to several we had recovered and disposed of.

"What is it?" Garrett asked as I took a step back. I stood on his foot in my efforts to back away from the object. "Ouch!"

"It's a tether," Aunt Thomasin explained. "Don't touch it, it could be poisoned. They're what the witch uses to the tie poison to her victims."

"So, she is poisoning Old Aggie!"

"It wasn't here when I visited the other day."

"Which means she is increasing her efforts."

I knocked on the door and waited but as no one answered a sense of dread enveloped me. "What if we're too late?"

Garrett rapped hard on the door. When the woman failed to reply, he stepped in front of the window and peered in. Net curtains obscured his view. "I can't see anyone, but it's difficult to tell."

After hooking the poison tether with a twig and lobbing it into the garden, I tried to open the front door. As expected, it was locked. "I'll go round the back," I said, searching along the row of terraces for the passageway to the back of the houses. A minute later I stood at the back of Aggie Sampson's house. The small garden was a neat and tidy display of raised beds although the herbs and vegetables growing within them had been left to overgrow in the past weeks.

"Poor woman," Aunt Loveday said. "Look at this mugwort! It is dying from thirst. She hasn't been out here for weeks by the look of these beds." Keeping herbs growing well, particularly those used in spells and charms was a point of pride for my aunts. Theirs were tended to daily, and reports on their health regularly bragged about in the kitchen over cups of tea. There were always bunches of something drying above the hearth. I peered into the kitchen. It was a small space filled with cabinets and open shelves. As at Haligern, bunches of herbs were hung to dry, but here they were attached to an old-fashioned clothes airer suspended to the ceiling. We had one at Haligern in the laundry room which also had a log burner. It was invaluable for getting clothes dry on those damp days when the sun couldn't do its job.

The sound of trickling water caught my attention and I noticed that the waste pipe at the back of the house was emptying water into the drain.

"She must be in there," I concluded. "There's a tap on somewhere in the house."

"Maybe she's upstairs then."

We agreed to wait, but as the water continued to run down the drain and there was no sign of Aggie Sampson ten minutes later, we decided to take action.

To my surprise, the back door was unlocked, and we stepped into the kitchen. I sensed the rot immediately.

"Stinks!" Aunt Thomasin hissed.

"Pooh! What is that smell?"

"Brimstone!" Aunt Thomasin explained.

The sulphuric stench was intense.

"The dark magick is working," she continued.

The downstairs comprised of a living room, dining room, and kitchen. It was a typical two up, two down built at the beginning of the late nineteenth century with the kitchen housed in a later, twentieth century, extension.

Aggie Sampson was not downstairs but what I did notice were the poison tethers that had been hung on each doorknob. "The witch has been in here! These weren't here when I visited before."

"Just don't touch them," warned Aunt Thomasin. "We'll collect them and destroy them before we leave."

Garrett took the lead, and we climbed the steep stairs to the bedrooms. We found Aggie in the first room we checked.

"Aggie!" Aunt Thomasin exclaimed.

On the floor, at the side of her bed, lay Aggie. From her sprawled form, it looked as though she had slipped from the bed. In her hand was a poison tether.

Her appearance was shocking and the voluminous, full length nightie with its long sleeves and ruffled collar, did nothing to hide her emaciated frame. Garrett crouched beside her, placing two fingers over her jugular. "She's alive," he confirmed. "Aggie! Can you hear me?"

Her mumbled response was indecipherable.

"She won't last much longer if we don't cleanse this house!" Aunt Thomasin said. "Livitha, remove the tether from her hand." She strode to the window, pulled the curtains apart and opened the window. "Fresh air for a start." She inhaled deeply and then turned to face the room. Ancient words began to flow as she lifted her arms as though in supplication. She seemed to grow in stature and the air coming in through the window began to blow around the room. My hair leapt, caught in a vortex of spiralling air.

I searched the room for something to protect my hand, removed an embroidered doily from the dressing table and plucked the tether from Aggie's hands. The effect was instant, and her eyes fluttered.

"Are you hurt?"

She sighed as though relieved of enormous pain.

"Don't move, Aggie. Let me lift you," Garrett instructed.

Lifting her with surprising ease Garrett lay her frail body on the bed. I covered her with a blanket then, as Aunt Thomasin continued to recite, worked my way through the house, collecting the tethers. With each tether found I recited the same charm I had used when collecting those around Haligern. In the kitchen I found a tin bucket and set the poisonous objects alight. With the tethers burning to ashes in the back yard I returned to the bedroom. The changed energy in the room was a relief. The stench of brimstone had receded, and Aggie was propped up with pillows and, though pale, had colour on her cheeks. Aunt Thomasin sat beside her on the bed, holding her hand.

"I can't believe I was so stupid!" Aggie exclaimed.

"Not stupid! It was a glamour. You were too weak to see through it, that is all."

"A glamour?" I asked.

"Yes. The tethers were encased in a glamour spell. They appeared to be what they were not. In the case of the one in Aggie's hand, it appeared to be a velvet pouch filled with herbs and was placed beneath her pillow to help her sleep. She realised within minutes that it was doing her harm, but by then it was too late."

"She was pulling it out from beneath her pillow when she fell."

Aggie nodded. "The sensation was terrible. I felt as though I were descending into the darkest of depths, as if I were slipping away to nothing!"

"Aggie. Who gave the tether to you?"

"Well, ... you will be shocked, but it was Celeste Driscoll!"

Chapter Twenty-Nine

The revelation that Mrs. Driscoll had placed the poison tether beneath Aggie's pillow, and probably placed the other tethers around the house came as a terrible shock. Worse was the knowledge that we had left her to care for Loveday and Raif on the evening of the wedding.

"That's why they were so ill the following morning!" I blurted. "When we left them to go to the wedding, they were getting better, their strength was improving, but the next day they were far worse! She did something!"

"I can't believe it's her!" Aunt Thomasin said. "It just doesn't make sense. She loves us."

"Does she?" I said remembering the look of malice she had cast me when Lina and I had talked in the shop. "I think there's a terrible streak of jealousy that runs through her."

"Livitha! How can you say that?"

The memories stirred up my own jealousies. "She's envious and greedy," I said. It had seemed so unfair to me that she should hog Lina's attention when it was so obvious that she wanted to be my friend too.

"I'm sorry, Livitha, but in all the time I have known Mrs. Driscoll I have never thought of her that way. She has always been so helpful and selfless."

"Well, then I think she has hidden a different side to her personality," I said in my defence. "Anyway, we should get back to Haligern immediately. She could still be there!"

We were all agreed that returning to Haligern was our next priority but first we had to make sure that Aggie was safe. Whilst Aunt Thomasin wrapped the house in a protective spell and made a herbal restorative from the ingredients in Aggie's kitchen, I found a neighbour who would be willing to sit with her for the next couple of hours. We exchanged phone numbers and I promised to call to check on her progress. I considered calling Dr. Cotta but decided against it. His attitude towards Uncle Raif's frailty had been to suggest hospitalisation and I knew that with time, in a cleansed home free of metaphysical poison, Aggie would soon recover. Plus, I now distrusted the doctor and, with his obsession of discovering witches, allowing him into Aggie's home could be disastrous for us all.

We were on the road within half an hour and headed back to Haligern.

"She's here!" I blurted as soon as we pulled into the driveway and spotted Mrs. Driscoll's small car, an immaculately polished red Volkswagen Polo. I opened my door as Garrett slowed to a stop.

"Steady on!" he warned as I unclicked my seatbelt.

Too impatient to wait, I flung open the door and jumped out before the car came to its final stop. I was rewarded with a twisted ankle and stumbled on the gravel, but quickly picked myself up then ran to the front door. It opened with difficulty but hadn't deteriorated any further than yesterday which gave me hope. The protective spells my aunts had cast were still working.

As car doors slammed behind me, I checked in the kitchen for my other aunts. "Where's Loveday?" I blurted.

"Upstairs! What is it? Whatever's happened?"

Without responding, I raced up the stairs to my aunt and uncle's bedroom. Here I did stop. I couldn't just barge into their room. A muffled 'Come in' followed my insistent knock. The door opened to a darkened room with that distinctive sulphuric smell. The rot was in here. Aunt Loveday was dressed but sitting in a large armchair close to the bed. She considered me with glazed eyes. Uncle Raif lay back against his pillows. I was thankful that he was asleep, seeing the lack of recognition in my aunt's eyes as I tried to speak to her was painful enough.

"What's going on?" she asked in a peevish voice. "Who are you?"

My gut twisted. "It's me, Aunt Loveday. Livitha."

"Oh." She smiled, nodded, stared at the closed curtains, then seemed to nod off all within the same second.

I scoured the room for tethers then checked beneath Loveday's pillow.

"Got you!"

Beneath the pillow was a woven circle of twigs with the same plaid fabric as the others. Without gloves, I improvised and removed the pillow from its case then pulled the case over my arm. With my hand now protected against any physical poison that it may be painted with, I picked up the tether and pulled my hand from the case. With the tether bagged, I turned my attention to Uncle Raif. He grumbled in his sleep as I made an effort to lift the pillow. Despite his frailty, his head was surprisingly heavy and, not wanting to wake him, but wary of touching the tether if it were there, I lifted the pillow with care.

There was nothing beneath. I breathed a sigh of relief, took a final look around the room in case any others had been placed there then returned to the kitchen.

"I found it!" I held the bag up in triumph.

"Found what?" Mrs. Driscoll had walked up behind me.

I swung to her, thrusting the bag in her face. "This!"

"A pillow case?" She looked alarmed, almost frightened.

Realising that I was being aggressive, I took a step back. "Yes! No. It's what's in the pillowcase."

"And what is in there?"

"You know what!"

"I do?"

"Liv, go steady." Garrett stepped beside me. "You're frightening the woman."

"Calm down, dear," Aunt Beatrice soothed. "And tell us what you found."

I swung back to my aunts. "It's a poison tether and Mrs. Driscoll put it beneath Aunt Loveday's pillow!"

"It's just a bag of lavender. I thought it would help her sleep."

"Sure!" My voice was laced with sarcasm. "Why don't you tell them what you really put underneath her pillow."

"A bag of lavender," she repeated.

Taking hold of the tether through the pillowcase, I pulled back the fabric to reveal the poisonous object. "Does that look like a bag of lavender?"

Gasps and hisses filled the kitchen as I held up the ring of woven twigs and bones.

"Whatever is that?"

Mrs. Driscoll seemed genuinely surprised, but I continued my confrontation. "Sure, play the innocent. You put it there. You know exactly what it is."

"Well, I never did put that ... thing under Loveday's pillow. Are those bones?"

"Yes, they are!"

Aunt Euphemia gripped my bicep and gently urged me to take a step away from Mrs. Driscoll. "Celeste. Who gave the bag of lavender to you?"

"Why it was ... now, let me think ... it was a ... a woman. She said that it would help Loveday sleep. You see I was explaining to her how poorly Loveday was – she was genuinely concerned for her health – and she gave me the bag to slip under her pillow before she slept. I put it there after you'd all gone to the wedding."

"And what did this woman look like?"

"Well, I ... I can't remember ..." Her eyes glazed and a dreamy smile came to her lips. "But I do like her. She's just such an interesting woman to talk to. So kind and funny and ... well, just lovely. I could spend all day talking to her."

"Hmm!"

Whispered murmurs filled the kitchen.

"If she's so wonderful, then tell us her name, and what she looks like," I demanded.

"Well ... isn't it odd. I just can't remember."

"That can't be true!" I blurted.

Mrs. Driscoll turned on me. "Are you calling me a liar?"

Feelings of resentment rose. "Yes!"

She narrowed her eyes.

I took a step forward. I wanted to scratch them out.

Aunt Thomasin waved her hand and Mrs. Driscoll froze, with her mouth partially open as she became statue-like mid-word.

"Well, sisters," Aunt Thomasin said, turning to my aunts, "it seems obvious to me what has happened."

"It is, sister," agreed Aunt Beatrice.

"Very clear, Thomasin," said Aunt Euphemia.

"As clear as mud!" My voice sounded disagreeable even to myself.

"Hegelina is using glamour to poison us. She has groomed Mrs. Driscoll and used her as a mule to get her poison into our house, just as she did with Aggie Sampson."

A wave of shame slid over me. I had been so rude to Mrs. Driscoll.

"But we're still no closer to knowing who she is! Mrs. Driscoll claims that she can't remember her."

"I think I know who she is. At least, who she's pretending to be."

All eyes turned to Aunt Euphemia.

"Mrs. Driscoll has talked a lot recently about a new friend. To be honest I've become absolutely sick of hearing about the woman."

"Oh, yes! Her new friend. She does seem to go on-"

"Ad nauseum!"

"So, who is it?"

"Her name is Lina."

"No!" I blurted. "It can't be her. She so nice."

All three aunts and Garrett turned to stare at me.

"She's got to Liv, too!"

The room grew silent.

"Well, it can't be her!" I said defensively. "She's such a wonderful person!"

"Wonderful, Liv?"

"Yes."

"And how often have you spoken to her?"

"And where?"

"At the shop. About twice," I admitted. "And I would have seen more of her if Mrs. Driscoll hadn't been so jealous of our friendship!"

"She's been compromised!" declared Aunt Beatrice.

"Oh, dear!"

"Livitha, tell us a little more about your special friend. You seem rather enamoured of her."

"Well, she is just so charming! She made me feel so ... at ease and ... and special."

"And you just wanted to spend time with her?"

"Yes!"

"Needed to be near her and listen to her talk?"

"Yes! She is fascinating. Oh, you should hear her talk about her travels and the people she has met, the places she has been. And she is *so* intelligent. Ask her anything ... and she knows. Such an interesting person."

"Hmm."

The aunts exchanged glances. A thought that they too wanted to get to know Lina crossed my mind and a small voice inside my head said 'She's my friend! Just mine!'

'*Yours. Just yours.*' The voice came from within me.

"Yes!" I whispered. "Mine."

"Liv?"

Chapter Thirty

The next minutes were the strangest I had ever experienced. Imagine being in a small space, an ultra-narrow lift, or one of those tiny WCs with only enough space for a toilet and a minute sink so close that you can wash your hands whilst you sit having a wee. Then imagine that you're sharing this space with another woman! That was the level of discomfort I suffered as Hegelina Fekkitt decided to project herself into my mind. I was seized by an intense sensation of simultaneous suffocation and claustrophobia. We were both crushed up against one another, with no room to move in the tiny toilet!

No longer in control of my own body, she began to speak and see through me. I tried to shout for help but was paralysed. Her eyes ranged over my aunts, Garrett, then Mrs. Driscoll frozen in time. She let out a deep and ugly cackle as she noticed the broken hearth. Turning her attention to my aunts she began to use my mouth, my tongue, and my vocal chords to speak.

I could only watch in horror as they listened to a torrent of venomous hate as Hegelina spewed insults and accusations. Garrett's bewilderment turned to a frown of anger. Aunt Thomasin grew pale, her face hardening.

It's not me!

Hegelina continued to rant.

It's not me! Don't listen to her!

No effort I made stopped Hegelina and I was only thankful that her power didn't extend to my arms and legs. She was murderous!

Bewildered shock quickly turned to cold stares. *Please! You've got to know this isn't me!*

Powerless to resist, the words continued to spew from my mouth. My aunts turned their backs and gathered in a huddle. Enraged, Hegelina ramped up her hate. Despite my inability to stop the rant, I watched my aunts closely. They were gearing up to retaliate.

As I noticed, so did Hegelina.

Forming a crescent, my aunts held hands and began to recite. Ancient words flowed. As the spell was cast, Hegelina jumped, leaving my mind in an instant. The spell hit and I was thrown back by its force, landing heavily against the large Welsh dresser. Jars clinked as the shelves shook then toppled. Several dropped, one smashed beside me, several others rolled across the floor spilling their contents, and another fell onto my head. A blast of pain rocketed through my skull.

Slumped against the dresser, agony filled my head and pain wracked every muscle, tendon, and bone in my body. "She's gone," I rasped as the pain faded to a deep and uncomfortable ache.

The kitchen was deathly silent.

All three aunts stood in watchful dread and only Garrett took tentative steps towards me. "Liv?"

Despite the heavy and dragging sensation that filled my body, I managed to hold out my hand. He offered me his.

"No!" Aunt Thomasin hissed. "Wait."

He pulled his hand back as though scorched. "But she's hurt."

"Yes, but we must be sure she is alone."

"I am," I managed. "She left before you cast the spell."

A low cackling filled the room and we all turned to the still frozen figure of Mrs. Driscoll. This time, the voice was coming from within her. Face contorted, mouth jawing with spiteful laughter, she was frightful.

"Did I look that terrifying?"

"Worse!" Garrett blurted.

"Oh, thanks!"

"You were like something possessed."

"Well, I was."

He shuddered as Mrs. Driscoll's eyes rolled to white. She continued to cackle.

"It's like some hideous horror film!"

"Poor Celeste," Aunt Beatrice said. "She will be mortified."

"Sisters, Hegelina must be ousted. You know what to do."

Once again, they formed a crescent and began to summon their ancient magick.

"Just hang on!" I blurted. "What if she just skips back into me?"

The recitation stopped.

"She has a point," said Aunt Euphemia.

"And what about Garrett? Could she jump into him?"

"Bloody hell! She can't, can she?"

"No. She hasn't groomed you for her purpose." Aunt Euphemia cast a sour, disapproving glance at Hegelina/Mrs Driscoll. "Her power only works over those she has ingratiated herself to, as she did with Liv and Mrs. Driscoll."

Garrett breathed a sigh of relief. "Good!"

"You must protect yourself from her, Livitha. Dig deep into your natural, ancestral magick," Aunt Thomasin instructed. "Create a barrier that she cannot pass if she tries to possess you again."

The aunts joined hands once more, forming a crescent close to Mrs. Driscoll. As I focused on drawing up my defences against the witch, Garrett slipped his hand into mine and gave it a reassuring squeeze. "You can do this, Liv."

The kitchen filled with voices. The screeching hate of Hegelina and the increasingly loud incantation of my aunts' magick. As their voices reached a crescendo, and they sent out the force of their cleansing magick, Mrs. Driscoll fell to the floor and I felt the power of Hegelina at the farthest boundary of my consciousness. I forced my mind to focus, bringing my energy to swathe me in its power, a resistant shield that sparked and fizzed each time she tried to penetrate. As though electrocuted, she recoiled with shock and pain each time her mind tried to push itself into mine. Words began to rise, and I recited them with strength. Hegelina raged and then, with a final screech of frustration, disappeared.

Chapter Thirty-One

A cup of tea laced with a calming elixir soothed Mrs. Driscoll's nerves as she recounted her ordeal. It was agreed that a spell of forgetfulness must be administered to the traumatised woman before she went home but not before she had given us as many details about Hegelina Fekkit as possible. She wasn't particularly helpful but at least she no longer effused about how wonderful the glamour witch was. However, from a previous conversation at the shop, I already knew where Hegelina lived.

With Mrs. Driscoll restored to her pre-possession self and on her way home, we sat at the kitchen table to figure out a plan of action.

"I say we go to her house now. We don't have any time to lose. As long as she's out there, she's poisoning Aunt Loveday and from the horrible things she was saying, I don't think she's going to give up on taking revenge any time soon."

"It sounded to me as though she hates you all. She could target all of you after tonight."

"I think that's exactly what she'll do."

"Then we have to find her and stop her."

"It's not as easy as that. She is a powerful witch, well-versed in the black magick arts and adept at disguising herself not to mention ingratiating herself into other people's psyche. She could have a whole army of protectors."

"She could, that's true, but we can't let that stop us."

"It won't, but we must have a plan."

"Indeed. We need our own weapons at the ready."

"I thought I saw her at Lady Annabelle's wedding, but then it wasn't her. It was odd."

"That was always her modus operandi—the ability to change appearance, or at least cast her glamour to hide herself."

"So how do we capture her if she's the mistress of disguise?"

"We can cast a discovery spell," Aunt Euphemia suggested.

"We could, but she'll be cute about it. She's intelligent enough to think ahead and cast her own spell against any discovery spell."

"Hmm ..."

"We'll cross that bridge when we come to it," said Aunt Thomasin. "As Livitha says, we have no time to lose."

"But if she does cast a hex against us then we could end up as ill and powerless as Loveday."

Discouragement crackled among my aunts as they began to brood on the difficulty of capturing Hegelina and decommissioning her powers.

"I have it!" I blurted as an idea sprang into mind. "Yes! It is exactly what we need."

"What?"

"Dr. Cotta!"

A communal groan filled the room.

"Not him, himself! But his witch detector."

Eyes lit up with interest.

"Ooh, yes! I'd forgotten about that."

"A witch detector! Are you serious?" asked Garrett.

"Yes! He really has one. He made it himself."

"And how do you know it works?"

"It detected me!" I said with joy.

"Hmm. Are you sure it wasn't just a stunt?"

"No. It was real. He's convinced we're witches. I insisted he was wrong, of course, but I don't think he believed me. That's why he's been so interested in me all this time. I'm pretty sure of that now."

Garrett's eyes lit up. "Good!"

"Good?"

"... Yes, it's good that he ... that he has a witch detector."

"It is, indeed."

"Well," said Aunt Beatrice. "What are we waiting for. Let's go and get it!"

Minutes later we piled into Garrett's car, each of us brimming with impatient anticipation. With Aunts Euphemia and Beatrice sliding onto the back seat Garrett started the engine. Sitting beside him, out on a mission to save my aunt and bring down our enemy, was truly thrilling. Part of the joy, I have to admit, was being able to sit so close to him.

Aunt Thomasin had reluctantly agreed to stay behind and take care of Aunt Loveday and Uncle Raif. In part this was because Aunt Beatrice insisted on coming with us. It was only fair, she said, that as Thomasin had already had an adventure that day, it was now her turn. It was also agreed that Thomasin's spell for protection was the most potent.

"We can't let him know that we're witches!" blurted Aunt Euphemia as the car began to roll forward.

I hadn't thought through quite how we were going to obtain the witch-finding device, just that I was going to obtain it. Obviously, our plan had a flaw.

"Well, what excuse are we going to use?"

"We can't just roll up there and ask for it. He will want to know what we want it for and, under no circumstances, can we tell him the truth," asserted Aunt Beatrice.

"I think he already knows!"

"Yes, but we can't be the ones to admit it!"

"But how else are we going to get it?"

"I can have it confiscated ..." Garrett suggested.

"But that would only arouse his suspicion."

"Not if he's suspected of bomb making."

"Well ... it did kind of look like it could be a bomb—it had wires and a flashing light ... but that's a bit extreme. I know you're not keen on him but making him out to be some sort of terrorist would ruin his career."

"Oh, we don't want to do that!" Aunt Beatrice said. "He may be a Cotta, but he's also a wonderful doctor. The word around the village is that he's doing marvels for people. I've heard such good things about him from Mrs. Driscoll."

Garrett mumbled something indistinct, and I sensed a wave of turbulent energy coming from his direction.

"She's right," added Aunt Euphemia. "He is a good doctor. I wouldn't want to see him come to harm, even if he is a snooping witch finder."

I had to agree. Despite Dr. Cotta's interest in discovering the coven's secrets, he had not made any indication that he wanted to do us harm. Still, we couldn't confirm that we were witches, even if his suspicions were correct.

"Well, we shall have to steal it then," I determined. "It's the only way."

"Break into his house?"

"Yes. He keeps it in his study. If I can get into the house, I can take it."

The idea wasn't met with enthusiasm, but no one offered an alternative method of retrieving the device.

"If we're successful-"

"That's a big 'if', Liv," Garrett said.

"Oh, I don't think it's so big," Aunt Beatrice disagreed. "We can use a cloaking spell to help her-"

"And an unlocking spell on the door, so we can get her in there-"

"Unseen." Aunt Beatrice giggled. "It will be such fun to take it from under his very nose!"

Aunt Euphemia shared her enthusiasm. "Indeed it will, sister."

"And once we've used it," I said, "we can put it back. He won't even know it was missing."

"Yes, but return it broken, so that it no longer works."

"So, that's agreed then. We borrow the device."

"Yes, that is exactly it. We borrow the device ... and then break it."

"Kill two birds with one stone."

"Stop a snoopy witch finder!"

Garrett grumbled something about breaking and entering but didn't make any real effort to convince us that it was a bad idea, and we continued our journey to the village. Parking around the corner from the surgery, it was agreed that Aunt

Euphemia should accompany me to the house to help with the lock.

I had only used magick to open a locked door once, and that had resulted in searing pain in my palm as though fire were burning through my skin, so I was quite happy to let Aunt Euphemia lead the way. Huge efforts had been needed on my part to unlock the door at the crematorium, but Aunt Euphemia managed this one with a few words and a stroke of the handle. I was impressed. "That was quick!"

She smiled and a twinkle shone in her eyes. "I know a few tricks."

The door opened with ease, and without any creak of its hinges, and we stepped through into the hall. We paused to listen, waiting for any hint of movement. The house was silent and, reassured that we hadn't woken Dr. Cotta, I brightened the space with a witch ball.

Loud wailing deafened me.

Startled, Aunt Euphemia covered her ears. "What is it?"

"House alarm!" I hissed. "Turn it off!"

"How?"

"With your magick. Quick!"

As the alarm continued to wail, I panicked. Dr. Cotta was sure to come down at any second, but I couldn't leave without the witch finder. Leaving Aunt Euphemia to deal with the alarm, I ran from the entrance hall and down the corridor that led to the study.

The alarm stopped. It had only sounded for seconds but it was a noise Dr. Cotta couldn't ignore. I had no more time to lose. I'd escape through a window if I had to.

I opened the study door and yelped.

Immediately in front of me, crowbar in hand and raised to strike, was Dr. Cotta.

"Liv!"

"Sorry!" Guilt, remorse, and shame hit me in an instant. No other words came to mind.

Anger softened to a bewildered frown. "What are you doing here?"

I glanced past him to the device on his desk.

"I ..."

He followed my glance. "Hah! You've come to destroy my witch finder."

"No!"

He held my gaze as I struggled to find a suitable excuse. I failed.

"Then what the hell are you doing breaking into my house ... And how did you manage to turn off the alarm?"

"I did it." Aunt Euphemia stepped out from behind me.

"Two of you!"

I nodded. I still had no idea what excuse I could give.

"Tell me what you're doing here, or I'll call the police!"

"There'll be no need for that." Garrett's voice boomed in the corridor as he appeared behind Aunt Euphemia. "The police are already here."

Dr. Cotta's eyes widened in surprise and he lowered the crowbar. "DCI Blackwood, isn't it?"

"That's correct, Dr. Cotta." Garrett's voice had an unfriendly edge to it.

Dr. Cotta's eyes narrowed. "Don't tell me that you came in response to my alarm going off, because I won't believe it. Coppers are never that quick."

As tension rose between the men I stepped further into the room. The witch finder was on the desk. I could take it whilst they were arguing.

"What are you doing here, Blackwood?"

Another step closer.

"That's DCI Blackwood to you, Dr. Cotta."

I stepped past Dr. Cotta.

"Sure! So ... what are you doing here DCI Blackwood?"

Cotta's hand shot out and wrapped around my bicep. The grip was firm but gentle. "Stay where you are, Liv." Dr. Cotta took a step back to the desk, blocking my view of the device, the crowbar raised once more. He took an aggressive stance.

"Oh, my!" exclaimed Aunt Beatrice as she appeared at the doorway. "This room is so clouded with tension, I can barely breath."

"Another one! Right. I demand to know exactly what you are doing here." He grabbed his phone from the desk and waggled it in the air. "You have ten seconds before I call the police. It's obvious that you're not here on official business Blackwood."

Aunt Euphemia sighed. "I knew this wouldn't work." As the eldest among us, she took charge. "We'd very much like to borrow your witch-detecting device."

All eyes fell on the box at the centre of the table. The lights were off and various tools were spread on the table. Dr. Cotta had obviously been working on the device.

Silence filled the room as he looked from the device to the group of house breakers. Bewildered anger turned to curiosity. "Tell me why and I'll consider it."

Chapter Thirty-Two

There was no choice. I had to tell Dr. Cotta the truth. Time was running out.

"We need it to find a witch!" I blurted.

The room grew silent as we watched Dr. Cotta's reaction. Momentarily, his eyes narrowed and then a broad smile split across his face. "Tell me more!"

"There's a witch in the village. She's using dark magick to poison my aunt. We know who she is, but she has the power to disguise herself-"

"Even to witches ... like yourself?"

His eyes locked to mine. Agreeing to his statement would be an admission that I was a witch. For several seconds I battled with myself. I was forbidden to reveal that I was a witch. Thankfully, Aunt Beatrice stepped into the breach.

"Yes," she said with authority. "Even for witches like ourselves."

"Hah!" Dr. Cotta crowed. "I knew it."

"Well, you won't know it soon," murmured Aunt Euphemia.

I realised then that they meant to erase Dr. Cotta's memory. We were safe. "Yes," I agreed, "Even to a witch like me."

Vindicated, Dr. Cotta released my arm and thumped the table. "I was right. Uncle Cotta was telling the truth. All of these years he has been mocked for his beliefs, but it was true!"

"He was right," Aunt Euphemia agreed. "And we can celebrate your victory later, but right now our beloved sister lays dying-"

"And Raif too," Aunt Beatrice added. "Your patient, Dr. Cotta."

"That's right!" I said. Despite his curiosity about witches, he was a doctor who cared deeply about his patients and I pushed those buttons. "My uncle, your patient, is dying, Dr. Cotta, he may not make it through the night. So, please, can we borrow your witch finding device?"

Dr. Cotta's triumphant smile faded as I spoke. He glanced at the device on the table. "If lending it to you save's your aunt and uncle's life, then of course. Please, take it."

Overcome with emotion, I threw my arms around his chest and hugged him but immediately released my grip. "Thank you!" I managed to blurt as I stepped back. "Sorry!"

Garrett grumbled beneath his breath.

"No need to apologise. I can see you're emotional right now."

I nodded. "I am."

"We've established that we're able to borrow the device," Garrett interrupted, "do you think we can progress to the next step and actually go and find this witch?"

Ignoring Garrett's snarky comment, Dr. Cotta retrieved the device from the table. With lights unlit, the device was obviously turned off. "Let's go!" he said with enthusiasm and a twinkle in his eyes.

"No!" Aunt Euphemia took a step forward and held out a hand for the device. "I'm afraid you won't be able to come with us, Dr. Cotta."

With a frown he pulled the device close. "Then you can't borrow it."

"You can't be serious?"

"I am." There was no doubting his determination.

However, Aunt Euphemia wasn't willing to back down. "Then we will just have to take it without your permission, Dr. Cotta!"

As sparks began to fly from her hands, and ancient words began to flow, Dr. Cotta raised the device. "Before you cast a hex on me-."

"Oh, it's not a hex, just a coercion spell, nothing to worry about—nothing harmful," soothed Aunt Beatrice with a smile.

The words continued to flow, and Aunt Euphemia raised sparking fingers.

"Well, before you cast a spell on me, let me show you something."

The flow of words stopped, and Aunt Euphemia dropped her hands. "Go ahead but be quick. We have no time to lose!"

Dr. Cotta sat the device on the table. "As you can see the device is currently switched off."

"Obviously."

"Well, when it detects magical power, the light becomes yellow. When it is on and there is no magical power, the light is green."

"So?"

"Please observe." He pushed a button on one side of the device. The light instantly shone yellow. "There!"

"So, it is yellow. That shows it is working."

Dr. Cotta shook his head whilst throwing me an indulgent smile. "What it's doing is showing that the people in this room have magical power."

"Yes …"

"Well, how are you going to detect a witch if when you're near it, it shows that it is detecting a witch?"

"Oh!" I said realising the implications. The machine would detect our magick as well as Hegelina's. It was useless.

"So … what shall we do?"

"Well, if I come with you then I can operate the device and detect the witch."

"What about Garrett?" I said. "He could use it."

Triumph extinguished from Dr. Cotta's eyes.

"Yes!" agreed Aunt Beatrice. "Give it to Garrett. He can operate it."

"I'm not sure-"

Aunt Euphemia waved a hand, muttering ancient words. Sparkles followed the arc of her hand and Dr. Cotta became silent, frozen in that moment. Aunt Euphemia breathed a sigh of relief then took the device from the table. "Everybody out," she commanded as she took steps to the door. "The spell won't last too long."

With a final glance at the statuesque Dr. Cotta I followed my aunts out of the house. The device glowed bright yellow.

"That was underhand, Euphemia!" said Aunt Beatrice.

"I know! But such fun!"

"Can I take that, please?" Garrett held out his hand for the device. "Before we go anywhere, we should check that it works. I'm still not convinced it isn't just a gimmick."

"A gimmick?"

"Yes. It could just be some elaborate party trick."

"A fake?"

"Yes, a fake. It would be easy to rig this up. A switch somewhere that Cotta could press when he wanted the lights to change. Schoolboy stuff." He huffed. "And anyway, what's more likely? That it really does detect magick, or that it is just a toy, an electronic prank?"

I suspected Garrett's doubts were based on underlying animosity to the doctor, but that the device could be a fake wasn't beyond the realms of possibility. He was right, a device that could be switched on and off at will was more likely than it being a real detector of magick.

"We must test it then," Aunt Beatrice said. "And quickly. He won't be frozen for many more minutes."

"Testing it should be easy enough. If I walk away from you all, then the light should go green. Is that right, Liv?"

I nodded. "That's what happened before. It was green until I stepped close to it."

"Good. So, I'll walk to the other side of the car park and it should go green." Without hesitation Garrett turned and walked to the far side of the carpark, which was at least fifty feet away from our position. When he turned to face us, the light shone yellow.

"It doesn't work!"

"It does." Dr. Cotta appeared in the doorway. He staggered and walked unsteadily towards Garrett. "Put the device on the ground," he instructed, "and I'll show you that it does."

Garrett placed the device on the ground.

Dr. Cotta raised his hands as though in surrender, palms splayed. "There's nothing in my hands. No buttons to press. No tricks!"

"He heard us!" Aunt Beatrice hissed.

"I have never known a spell to last such a short time!" Aunt Euphemia glanced at her hands. "I think Hegelina may be casting her poison on me!"

"Now go back to stand with the ladies, DCI Blackwood," Dr. Cotta instructed.

"Fine!"

As Dr. Cotta continued to hold his arms aloft, Garrett walked towards us. At about ten feet from the device, the light began to flash and then changed to green.

"It's not yellow!" Aunt Beatrice said.

"What does it mean?"

Dr. Cotta stooped to pick up the device. Held it aloft to show the green light still glowing then walked towards us.

At about ten feet away, the light began to flash and then became a solid yellow.

"It means," said Dr. Cotta, with a broad smile, "that DCI Blackwood is also emitting an energy my device can detect."

"Hereditary magick still runs through his veins," confirmed Aunt Euphemia. "Even if the family is banished."

Garrett frowned and in a grudging voice said, "We'll have to take Dr. Cotta with us."

"It's the only way you'll catch a witch tonight!" Dr. Cotta beamed.

Chapter Thirty-Three

The drive to Hegelina's cottage was awkward. Dr. Cotta had asked that I join him, and it felt churlish to refuse. Despite efforts to appear nonchalant, Garrett's jaw had clenched as I'd agreed. With the witch-finding device switched to off and safely on my lap, we set off for the cottage, following Garrett's lead.

Discovering Dr. Cotta's witch-finding device had uncovered his true intentions towards me. I felt relieved but also embarrassed. Of course, he didn't really like me. What man, built like an Adonis, would?

A blurted accusation broke the awkward silence. "So ... all this time you've just been digging for information about my family and the coven," I said, unable to keep the accusatory tone out of my voice.

A quick glance from his brilliant blue eyes made me squirm. "Do you really think I'm that shallow?" he threw back at me.

"Well, why else would you want to take me out? It's obvious that you're obsessed with proving your uncle right."

"It's not like that, Liv."

"Really? I find that hard to believe. I'm over fifty and not exactly-"

"Just stop right there!"

That look again!

"I asked you out because … because I liked you."

I didn't believe him. "So my family's magick had nothing to do with it?"

"No!" He grew quiet, then said. "Let me be absolutely honest. Sure, learning more about you and your aunts was a draw, but I honestly do like you. You're funny, quirky, interesting. You've made being here a little less lonely and a heck of a lot more entertaining."

"Well-"

"And I can't wait to get to know you all a whole lot better."

He was genuine, but it was obvious that he was less interested in me romantically than he was discovering more about our witchcraft. Anyway, it was a moot point; once this was over my aunts would erase his memory and most certainly disable his witch-finding device.

Garrett's car slowed and pulled over to the kerb. Hegelina's cottage was just beyond the village boundary. A detached cottage surrounded by gardens separated from the nearest house by a paddock, it was surrounded by overgrown hedges—the perfect place for a witch to work in peace and quiet.

Leaving the streetlights behind, we walked down the narrow lane to within fifty feet of the cottage.

Hairs rose on my neck and I felt the sensation of waves of dark energy lapping at my skin.

"I can feel her!" Aunt Euphemia whispered.

"Me too. I thought it was just me."

"No, I feel it too."

"We know, then, that she's inside."

With dark power emanating from the cottage, we stood in a cluster, increasingly agitated. My thoughts became scattered and then her voice rose in my mind. She was forcing her way in, trying to see through my eyes as though she were standing at a window twitching the curtains. I snapped my eyes shut and pushed back at the probing fingers of her mind. Around me, I could still hear the others talking. Garrett and Dr. Cotta were arguing about our next steps. A hand gripped my elbow and Aunt Beatrice stood beside me, her thoughts joining mine. 'Out, damned witch! Out!'

My mind closed against the glamour witch as though a steel trap door had snapped shut. "She was trying to get into my mind again!" I gasped.

"She's gone now," Aunt Beatrice whispered.

"Does she know we're here?"

With a sweep of Aunt Euphemia's hand, and a murmur of magical words, a shimmering and iridescent dome rose to cover us. She swayed, the effort of creating the protective dome sapping her energy.

"There," she said. "This will protect us from her spying eyes, but we must hurry. I can feel my energy draining and hers growing."

"She has turned her attention to *us*, sister," Aunt Beatrice said. "If she succeeds, then the coven will be lost ..."

"I'm going in," Dr. Cotta declared.

"Going in?" Garrett asked in a near-mocking voice.

Ignoring the slight, Dr. Cotta held up the device and switched it on. The light flashed and then became solid yellow. "We have to confirm it's her, don't we?"

Garrett replied with a 'Yes!'

"Then I'll go to the house and confirm it is her."

Suddenly afraid for Dr. Cotta, I grabbed his arm "But there's nothing to protect you."

He placed his hand over mine. "I'm just going to knock on the door—I'm new around here and I've lost my way, got the wrong address. She won't know anything."

"Don't go into the house," warned Aunt Beatrice.

"I won't."

"You really mustn't. Whatever she says, don't go into the house."

"Don't worry. I'm just going to knock on the door."

Dr. Cotta stepped out of the protective dome and walked along the narrow lane to the cottage.

"Come on," I urged. "We have to see."

With the dome surrounding us as we made our way to the house, we stopped at the front gate. Dr. Cotta was standing beneath the front porch. Large roses filled the trellis and grew over its pitched roof. Soft light shone from the windows. A gap in the curtains showed a living room complete with open fire where Hegelina sat on the sofa reading a book. I became doubtful. She was just a woman reading a book and there was nothing unusual about that. For the seconds before Dr. Cotta knocked on the door, I watched her and became overwhelmed by the sadness of loss. I had so wanted her to be my friend!

With her attention drawn by the knocking on her front door, she placed the book down and disappeared from view. The light on the witch-finding device changed from green to flashing yellow. The door opened and the light became solid. Illuminated by the hallway light, Dr. Cotta introduced himself to the witch standing in the doorway. Seconds passed. He laughed, she smiled, and then he stepped into the house.

Chapter Thirty-Four

"He's gone inside!"

"Obviously!"

"I told him not to!"

"We have to get him back!"

For several seconds we stood in shock.

"She's locked the door!"

"She always was a maneater! I wouldn't be surprised if she hasn't got a whole harem of men in that house."

Garrett and I exchanged glances.

"True. She always was something of a cougar," agreed Aunt Beatrice. "That's why she's so adept at using her glamour. If the men weren't interested in her natural charms, then she turned on her glamour."

"I think that's why Loveday was so keen to have her exiled."

I listened to the conversation in fascination whilst still watching the house. The main light in the living room was replaced by flickering candlelight. Perhaps my aunts were right and Hegelina was seducing Dr. Cotta with her glamorising magick!

"She did nearly lose Raif."

The mention of my uncle's name added an extra depth to my interest in Hegelina's powers. "How did Aunt Loveday nearly lose Raif?"

"Is this really necessary, ladies?" Garrett butted in. "Shouldn't we be discussing our next steps."

"Oh, yes, but it will only take a moment to explain about Raif."

Garrett gave an indulgent sigh whilst glancing at the house then turned back to listen.

"Well, Hegelina set her sights on Raif—this is back during the time when the romance between Loveday and Raif was just beginning to deepen-"

"That's correct, Beatrice. Well, Hegelina – she had always been jealous of Loveday – decided that she wanted Raif for herself and set about capturing him."

"She was a great beauty in those days!"

"Well, despite her 'great beauty', Raif held true and was loyal to Loveday."

"Hegelina hated that!"

"She did, Beatrice. So, enraged at his rejection, she began to use her glamour upon him."

"And one night she stole Raif away!"

"Stole him away?"

"What Beatrice means is that one night, her magick had become so powerful that Raif became spellbound-"

"He walked to her home in a lovesick trance!"

"Ladies, can we listen to the rest of the story later, please? Dr. Cotta may need our help?"

"Yes, yes, but listen one moment more. Well, thankfully, Loveday intercepted Raif just as he was about to enter Hegelina's cottage."

"And she saved him?"

"Yes, and she saved him, but if he had entered all would have been lost."

"Ooh! Loveday was so angry when she discovered Hegelina's deceit."

"Yes, and that is why, when she got the chance, she relished being able to send the woman into exile."

Candlelight flickered in Hegelina's front room. "Do you think that Dr. Cotta is lost, then?"

"I doubt it. She hasn't made a concerted effort to obtain him in the way that she had with Raif."

"Okay," said Garrett. "Now that we've heard the story of Raif's near miss with this man-eating ancient cougar-witch, can we make a plan for just how we're going to stop her?"

"Well, it's quite simple. We know that she is inside the house, so Beatrice and I will confront her."

I know it was cowardly, but a wave of relief washed through me. After having the creeping tendrils of Hegelina's mind inside my own, the last thing I wanted was a battle with the witch.

"Let's go then," Garrett urged.

Still protected beneath the magical shield we walked up to the cottage. Inside the front room I caught sight of Dr. Cotta leant against the hearth contemplating the fire then Hegelina passing him a glass of wine. For a captive, he seemed quite happy!

Again, I grew concerned that we were targeting the wrong woman. Could my Lina really be the same monstrous creature that had invaded my mind and was poisoning Aunt Loveday? A hand gripped my bicep, the fingers digging down into the muscle.

"Ow!"

"She is one and the same, Livitha!" Aunt Beatrice scolded.

I realised then that I was once again being entranced by Lina's glamour. Each time I saw her, I felt drawn to her. I shuddered and forced myself to concentrate on the task in hand—defeating Hegelina Fekkitt to save my aunt and uncle.

"Are we just going to knock on the door?" I whispered.

"Yes."

"And then what?"

"We lure her out."

"And then we bind her."

"And that's it? As simple as that?"

"Yes," Aunt Euphemia answered and rapped on the door. "Now, step back into the shadows and let me work."

We shuffled back into the shadows along the side of the house. Aunt Euphemia flicked her hand in our direction and the air grew opaque.

The door opened casting light on my aunt. She smiled, nodded, and then stepped through the door.

I lurched forward but was instantly blocked by Garrett who held me back until the door closed. "What just happened?" I hissed.

"She's onto us!" Aunt Beatrice hissed back.

"No kidding!" I retorted. Dismayed at my aunt's disappearance into the witch's lair, I turned to Garrett. "What do we do?"

"I'll talk to her," Aunt Beatrice suggested.

"No! She'll just draw you in like she did Aunt Euphemia."

"Liv's right," Garrett said. "This isn't working."

"Well, how are we going to stop her?"

"We have to catch her unawares," Aunt Beatrice said.

"And just how do you suggest that we do that?"

"By getting into the house without her knowing and catching her off-guard," explained Aunt Beatrice. "We have been naïve! Being upfront has not worked. We have to be as sneaky as she is."

I scanned the cottage. "The back door?" I suggested. Aunt Beatrice shook her head. Where else was there? "The chimney?"

"Tsk! No. We can go through an upstairs window."

"And just how are we going to do that?" Garrett asked.

"I can look for a ladder?" I suggested.

"No need," Aunt Beatrice. "We can elevate ourselves."

"Oh! Of course," I said, realising that she meant we could fly. There were several garden implements with long handles propped up against the garden shed. I gestured to them. "Should I get a yard brush, or a hoe?"

"No need," she repeated and began to rise.

Slack jawed, Garrett and I watched as my diminutive aunt rose to the level of the upstairs windows. Pink, blue, and purple sparks flashed as she moved her hands in an upward motion. Obediently, the sash window opened. "Come on then!" she hissed then disappeared inside.

"You'd best do as she tells you, Liv."

"But ... I can't!"

"She thinks you can," Garrett replied.

Aunt Beatrice leant out of the window. "Hst! Come on."

I focused on my magic but was rewarded with nothing. "I can't!" I whispered as Garrett urged me to try.

"Let me help," he said.

"How can you he-eelp!"

Before I had a chance to reject his offer, he crouched, clasped both arms around my knees and, with a grunt of effort lifted me up. Straining, he said, "There you go, now fly up!"

"Put me down!" I hissed, horrified.

"No!" His voice was strained. "You've got to go up!"

Realising that he was more likely to suffer a hernia than let me down, I focused my energy. I had never tried elevating, didn't even know it was a thing until a few seconds before, but I engaged the same part of my core that seemed to enable flight. My hands sparked, more from intense embarrassment than the revving up of magical powers, but to my amazement, Garrett's arms changed from holding me up to holding me back. "Okay," I said. "I think you can let me go."

"Hst!" berated Aunt Beatrice. "Come on!"

Garrett released my legs and I hovered. There was nothing ladylike about my effort. I swayed and wobbled like a giant weeble, flapping my arms to keep me centred but, within seconds, I had reached the bedroom window. Aunt Beatrice stepped back, beckoning me inside as though she were landing a plane. I was more of a lumbering cargo plane than a nimble spitfire but by some miracle I managed to squeeze through the window and land in the bedroom without crashing to the floor. Aunt Beatrice immediately held a finger to her lips. "We'll go downstairs and surprise her in the living room," she said.

"That can't be the plan!" I complained.

"What else do you suggest?"

"Well, something a little more solid than 'we'll surprise her in the living room.'"

"Go ahead, Livitha. I'm all ears," she retorted.

It was then that we heard the groan from the bed!

Chapter Thirty-Five

Aunt Beatrice clutched my bicep, fingers squeezing to a pinch. Ignoring the pain, I clasped her hand and we both turned to face the noise.

In the failing light we could only make out a lump in the middle of the bed. Movement was accompanied by another groan and then a snort followed by the sucking of air. I felt my own chest tighten as I held my breath then released it as the body on the bed breathed out with another long and nasal snort.

"It's a man!" Aunt Beatrice hissed.

"He's asleep!" I replied.

In the failing light, apart from the large mound of cloth-covered body, it was difficult to make out the figure on the bed. I lit a witch light, holding it in my flattened palm. Since my first use of this magical form of illumination, I had become adept at controlling it and could now brighten its energy at will. Set to dim, I increased the brightness as the man continued to snore, oblivious to us.

"Who is it?" Aunt Beatrice whispered. "Is it Cotta?"

"Unlikely."

"Well look then!"

Aunt Beatrice had taken to being quite feisty since Aunt Loveday had become ill and I wasn't sure I was very keen on this newly empowered aunt. "Give me a minute!" I hovered over the figure. All that could be seen of the man beneath the duvet were a few hairs.

"He's got greyish hair," I reported.

"Pull the covers back."

I huffed. Pinching the edge of the cover, I peeled it back from the man's face. He looked familiar.

"Well? Who is it?"

"I don't know. You take a look."

Aunt Beatrice took a step forward, raised herself onto tiptoes then peered down at the snoring man. "Tarquin Sotheby-Jones!"

The stolen bridegroom! "No way!"

He snorted, shifted in the bed then let out a long and sonorous fart.

"Oops!" Aunt Beatrice said.

My laughter was instant, but I held it in, shoulders heaving. Aunt Beatrice pulled me back from the bed as Tarquin snorted again and then began to mumble in his sleep. A noxious aroma arose from the bed.

We took another step away.

Aunt Beatrice held a hand over her nose. "Well ... at least we know he's alive," she whispered, then pulled me towards the door.

"He smells as though he's dead!" I quipped.

"Now, be sensible, Livitha!" she scolded as I repressed another fit of laughter.

We stood at the door, the farthest from the sleeping man as we could get in the small room. I re-lit the witch light and then, startled, held my breath again. In the corner of the room stood another figure. I stood transfixed and rigid as the woman stared across the room. She didn't move and it took several, heart-pounding seconds before I realised the terrifying woman was a mannequin. Its eyes glinted, and illuminated by my witch light, diamonds twinkled and glittered around her throat. "The Heskitt Inheritance!"

"She did steal them!"

Tarquin mumbled again in his sleep, this time calling out Lina's name.

"Do you think he's in on it too?" I asked.

"I don't know," Aunt Beatrice replied, "but he seems to be rousing!"

I extinguished the light just as Tarquin's eyes flickered open.

Unnoticed, the mannequin's eyes dulled.

"Lina? Come to bed," he muttered. "I've been waiting for you." Still half asleep, he threw the cover back in an open invitation. We took that as our cue to escape.

"Cheating miscreant!" Aunt Beatrice said as the bedroom door shut with a soft click behind us.

"He's under her spell," I said.

"Hah! A likely story!"

"Anyway," I whispered, "forget about him." I motioned for her to follow me to the top of the stairs, my confidence buoyed at having found Tarquin and the jewels.

Thankfully, the stairs were carpeted, and we took soft steps down to the main entrance hall where light shone from beneath the living room door.

I unlocked the front door to allow an easy escape.

Muffled laughter came from the living room.

"This is it!" I said. "We go in and ..."

The door swung open to reveal Dr. Cotta. Towering above me, he smiled. "Liv! Come on in." Taken aback, I hesitated. "Aunt Bea!" he exclaimed and held up a nearly empty glass of wine. "Join us!" Despite his enthusiasm, his eyes were glazed.

"He's under a spell," I said.

He took a step back from the doorway to allow us to enter. With any hope of surprising Hegelina gone, I stepped inside the room. Aunt Euphemia was seated beside the fire, bound to the chair by a string festooned with tethers. She was gaunt, frail, and withered.

"Euphemia!" Aunt Beatrice gasped and rushed to her side but withdrew as though stung as she touched the string.

The witch-finding device had been placed on a small table in the corner of the room and flashed yellow, no doubt picking up on our energy. Hegelina was nowhere to be seen.

"Where's Lina?"

"Dunno," replied Dr. Cotta and held his glass aloft before slugging the remaining wine and pouring himself another glass. "Have a glass, Liv! The party has only just started." He took another slug of wine and then began to sway as though hearing music.

Aunt Euphemia groaned.

"We have to untie her, Livitha. She's so weak!"

As I agreed and took a step towards the pair, I noticed that a change had overcome Aunt Beatrice. The glow had disappeared from her cheeks and they were sallow and sunken. "Move away from her, Aunt Bea! The tethers are poisoning you too!"

She managed a staggering sidestep. "Now, let me think ... there must be a spell I can use ..."

With dismay, I realised that Aunt Bea was struggling to remember her magick. In a moment of mutual understanding, she caught my eyes. "You're going to have to overcome her, Livitha," she said in a voice cracked with age. "Find her and destroy her!"

From somewhere in the house, Hegelina cackled. She was destroying *us* with her magick and enjoying every minute. I had to find her and put a stop to her vengeance.

"Go, Livitha!" Aunt Beatrice sank to the floor, her face already wizened.

Dr. Cotta stood mute. Spellbound by the witch, he was useless to me. A cackle erupted from another room and this time it sounded as though it were coming from upstairs.

With my aunts out of action, I was the only one left who could confront Hegelina's dark magick and I had no idea where to start.

"Destroy the glamour!" Aunt Beatrice croaked and then slumped against a chair.

'Destroy the glamour'. The phrase repeated in my head.

"Livitha!" Hegelina called in a mocking tone. "Oh, Livitha!" she sang. "Are you coming out to play?"

I swung in the direction of the voice. It seemed to come from the hallway, but as I turned, the space was empty. Another cackle. I followed the noise, stepping out of the living room checking for Hegelina on the stairs or in the hallway. With no sign of the woman, and her call repeating from above, I moved towards the stairs. It was then that I noticed a figure standing in the kitchen doorway at the end of the hall. Heart hammering, I realised it was Dr. Cotta.

But he was behind me—in the living room!

The hairs on my neck rose as Cotta took a step towards me. Hegelina's cackling laugh echoed and I could no longer tell whether it came from upstairs, behind Cotta, or even outside.

I glanced back into the living room. Sure enough, Dr. Cotta stood with zombie-like placidity although his eyes had lost their glazed appearance. I returned to the Cotta in front of me. It too was zombie-like. It took a step toward me, hands outstretched like two massive claws.

"Stop right there!" I hissed holding out a defensive palm.

"Li-i-v!" it croaked. "Li-i-v!"

It took another step forward. Whatever it was, this wasn't *the* Dr. Cotta.

Behind me, the other Cotta stepped forward. "Liv!" he said. "What's going on?" Relieved, I took a step away from the zombie-like Cotta and towards the Cotta in the living room. Zombie-Cotta took a lurching step forward, and made a strangling noise. I slammed the door shut. Hegelina's cackling laugh erupted again.

Eyes now cleared of their dullness Dr. Cotta seemed almost back to normal as he stared down at me. The dark magick had worn off.

"Thank goodness you're back!" I said whilst searching his face for any sign that he was still under her spell.

"Me too!" He shuddered as though shaking off a chill. "It was weird, being under her control."

"I know. It's freaky," I empathised. "She did it to me too!"

"Where is she?"

"I'm not sure. Her voice sounds as though it's coming from upstairs, but then there's a zombie-style replica of you in the hallway!"

"That is something I've got to see," he said and stepped towards the door.

"No!" I barred his way. "You have no protection against her. I'll find her, but first let's help my aunts." Both aunts were still suffering under Hegelina's magick and, knowing that he wouldn't be poisoned by the tethers in the same way that my aunts were I instructed him to remove them using a cushion cover as a protective 'glove'.

It was as he stood at the end of the sofa pulling the inner cushion from its velvet case that I noticed the light on the witch detecting device. It had changed from flashing yellow to solid.

Hiding my surprise, I turned to tend to Aunt Beatrice.

The yellow light changing from flashing yellow to solid meant only one thing. The device had picked up on a strong witch energy which meant that this Cotta wasn't Cotta at all. Zombie-Cotta was the real Cotta, and he was trapped behind the door shuffling and groaning like the undead. This Cotta was Hegelina camouflaged by her glamour magick!

I made a fuss of helping Aunt Beatrice into a more comfortable position as I made frantic efforts to think of my next move.

I had only precious seconds.

Ugly. That had been Aunt Beatrice's last word. It repeated in my mind. *Ugly*. Ugly was the opposite of what Hegelina strived for. To be ugly was to be repugnant, the very opposite of how she wanted to be seen.

Ugly!

Ugliness was the antidote to glamour.

Think, Liv, think!

I forced my thoughts to consider what was ugly. Pascal as a toad was certainly ugly. My thoughts jumped to Haligern. Nothing there was ugly, apart from-

"There, done it!" Cotta/Hegelina took a step towards me.

As its foot pressed down into the carpet, I sprang into action, throwing my hands out and hitting it with a blast of energy. Magick leapt from my fingers as a powerful bolt of lightning. Sparks flew and Cotta was flung back against a bookcase. Taken by surprise, the witch's disguise disappeared, and it was Hegelina who faced me. She looked similar to the woman who had called herself Lina, but with the glamour gone, so had the prettiness of her face. In front of me was a hag with an aura of hate-fuelled energy and spite-filled eyes.

Ugly!

She is, I silently agreed.

Curse her!

Hegelina began to pull herself up, a snide smirk already replacing the shocked grimace. I had to act now!

The words spilled from my mouth in a torrent, ancient words rising from an ancestral core.

"Evil witch full of spite,

Now shall I put you right,

Your foul magick, I bind it in a knot,

I toss it in the pit, where it shall rot,

Re-formed,

Transformed,

With curling horns,

With cloven hooves,
With swollen udder,
An ugly beast to make men shudder,
Bound to Haligern Coven, you will live your days as a goat eternal!

Hegelina Fekkit, I give you the kiss of my curse infernal."

With the last word out of my mouth, I blew her a cursed kiss. Particles of magick shimmered in the air, reeling and eddying as they sped towards her in an intense cloud. Holding form for an instant the cloud then exploded to rain the curse down upon her.

With a furious shriek, she began to transform.

She shrank, her body twisting and contorting as it reshaped. Back curving, legs and arms extending, hands and feet melded to form hooves. Two lumps appeared on her forehead and quickly grew to mounds that sprouted horns. Her eyes remained dark blue, but the pupils elongated to form a lozenge. She spat and hissed as her small white teeth became yellowed, and broadened, filling her mouth whilst her jaw simultaneously elongated stretching her nose to a flattened expanse. Hairs sprouted on her top lip and below her chin. Contorted and stretched by her new shape, her clothes split to reveal a thick layer of white hair and, as foot-long horns curled around her now elongated and hair-tipped ears, she began to bleat.

Chapter Thirty-Six

The flash from Dr. Cotta's mobile phone caught me by surprise and I was momentarily blinded as I tugged Hegelina down the pathway. Like any old goat, she was stubborn. Aunt Euphemia, on the other side of the recalcitrant witch, held tight to the rope we'd managed to lasso around her neck. Scavenged from her living room curtains, the jute tiebacks, complete with fringed tassels, were perfect for the job. Behind us Garrett, the *Heskitt Inheritance* safely in his jacket pocket, walked with a tight grip on a handcuffed Tarquin Sotheby-Jones.

As Hegelina had begun to bleat, the kidnapped bridegroom had charged downstairs. Disturbed by the commotion, and now fully awake, he had blundered into the living room in a peacock print silk kimono that was unflatteringly short and only just wrapped across his rounded belly. Bewildered by our presence he had demanded to know where Lina was.

Determined to discover whether he had been under her spell or a willing accomplice, I had lied and told him that she had popped out to the shops. Obviously, there was no easy explanation as to why a goat was in her living room, but he seemed to swallow my story that Lina was interested in buying a goat and we'd brought it round for her to take a look at. I kept a straight face as I spoke and watched as his bemused frown changed to one of confused acceptance.

Keeping my eyes above shoulder level, I began my interrogation. With my questioning cloaked as casual conversation, I quickly discovered that Tarquin and Lina were betrothed and planning to marry the following month. A small ceremony in a Registry office in the nearby town followed by a two-week honeymoon on the Cote D'Azur had been arranged. With Lina now cursed, and her magick void, it became obvious that he wasn't under her spell, but a willing accomplice.

When Tarquin had asked to be excused in order to dress more appropriately then disappeared upstairs, I took the opportunity of fetching Garrett. Ten minutes later, Tarquin was handcuffed and under arrest for the theft of Lady Heskitt's jewellery.

As we dragged Hegelina through the gate, a police car drew up to the curb. Two officers stepped out, bundled Tarquin into the backseat then, after a short conversation with Garrett, drove off again.

Another flash blinded me as I turned to Garrett.

"No one will believe this!" Dr. Cotta said as he took yet another photograph, this time one of my Aunt Beatrice.

"You are correct, Dr. Cotta," Aunt Euphemia replied. "They won't." With a wave of her hand that was followed by sparks, she looked him in the eye and said, "Whenever you try to convince someone that you saw witches, you will speak only gobbledygook and people will assume you are losing your marbles!"

"But I did see them!" he insisted. "And they do exist!"

"Yes, but you can't tell people that!" I explained.

"But you *are* all witches," he said, "and I saw you transform that woman into a goat! That's proof." He held up his mobile. "Here's proof!"

"The spell hasn't worked," quipped Garrett. "Should I confiscate his phone?"

"No way!" Dr. Cotta shoved his phone deep into the front pocket of his jeans.

"There's no need," said Aunt Euphemia. "I've taken care of it."

"But the spell hasn't worked!" complained Garrett. "He's still talking about seeing witches and having photographic proof."

"Pish!" blurted Aunt Beatrice. "He has photographs of a bunch of old women and a goat. That's proof of nothing."

"Aunt Beatrice is right," I said. "He didn't take any photographs of Hegelina transforming. He was zombified in the hallway when it happened."

"But my device worked! And I was put under a spell by a witch! That's proof enough."

Aunt Euphemia sighed. "That may be so, but no one will believe you."

"Of course they will." He held up his witch-finding device. "And I can prove it with this!"

"I hate to say it again," said Garrett, "but I don't think the spell has worked. I can still understand him."

"Oh, it has," Aunt Euphemia corrected. "He can talk to us, I wouldn't be that cruel, but to anyone else, what he utters will be sheer gibberish."

It took us another twenty minutes to bundle Hegelina into the back of Garrett's car. This time, my aunts rode with Dr.

Cotta whilst I sat on the backseat doing my best to keep Hegelina under control.

Back at Haligern, with Hegelina now safely in the pen, I leant against the wooden fence with Garrett at my side and watched as Old Mawde eyed her new roommate warily. The two cursed harridans circled one another for several minutes and then stood at opposite ends of the pen in an aggressive stand-off.

"Do you think they'll get along?"

"I'm not sure that they will," I replied as Old Mawde took a step forward. Hegelina shifted her position, backing up to the fence. "But they'll have plenty of time to get to know each other. I think I cursed her for eternity, or forever, something like that."

Garrett sighed and I sensed a change in his energy. His face was sombre as he turned to me. "Liv," he said, "I was just ..."

"Livitha! Garrett! There's a cup of tea waiting for you," Aunt Beatrice shouted from the kitchen doorway. "Don't be long, or it will be cold!"

"We'd best go in," Garrett said taking a step towards the house.

I grabbed his arm. "No! Please, finish what you were going to say."

"Well ..." he took my hands in his, rubbing mine gently with his thumb. "I was just wondering if-"

"Livitha!" shouted Aunt Beatrice. "Quick there's something in the kitchen you must see!"

"Tea *and* 'something in the kitchen'—they really want you back in the house!"

"The tea can wait," I said irked that they were making it so obvious they didn't want us to talk alone.

"But the 'something' could be important," Garrett suggested and took a step towards the house. His mood, like mine, seemed to have taken a downward turn.

"It is," Aunt Beatrice said suddenly by my side.

Startled, I yelped. "Don't do that!" I scolded.

"Sorry, dear, but after discovering Hegelina's tricks in the woods, I've decided to brush up on my transporting skills. They were quite rusty!"

"Still-"

"Now, come along. You really must see what's in the kitchen."

"What is it?"

"It's just been delivered."

"But I haven't ordered anything."

"Oh, it's not from any kind of shop."

"Come and see. It's a delivery from the other realm. Quite mysterious."

"But what is it?"

"A locked box."

"But who sent it?"

"Tsk! So many questions. Come along. It's addressed to you and we're dying to know what's inside."

The End

Discover the secret of the box in 'Midlife Hexes & Gathering Storms'[1]

1. https://www.amazon.com/dp/B0919SRFYH

JC's Reader Group

Dear witchy mystery fan!

I'd love to stay in touch. To receive bonus content and writing updates, please sign up to my reader group. You can join via my website, or Facebook. Once you join please download my gift to you.

Reader Group: https://dl.bookfunnel.com/pgh4acj6f8
Website: www.jcblake.com[1]
Facebook: www.facebook.com/jcblakeauthor[2]

---

1. http://www.jcblake.com

2. http://www.facebook.com/jcblakeauthor

Other Books by the Author

Menopause, Magick, & Mystery
Mysteries of the witchy variety featuring mature women proving life can be a wonderful adventure after fifty!
Hormones, Hexes, & Exes[1]
Hot Flashes, Sorcery, & Soulmates[2]
Night Sweats, Necromancy, & Love Bites[3]
Menopause, Moon Magic, & Cursed Kisses[4]
Midlife Hexes & Gathering Storms

Marshall & Blaylock Investigations
If you love your mysteries with a touch of the supernatural then join ghost hunting team Peter Marshall and Meredith Blaylock in:
When the Dead Weep[5]
Cawbrook Farm[6]

---

1. https://books2read.com/u/4A7pJe

2. https://books2read.com/u/baaXg2

3. https://books2read.com/u/mldwMA

4. https://books2read.com/u/3LYkD1

5. https://books2read.com/u/bwdyA0

6. https://books2read.com/u/3GdV7L

Printed in Great Britain
by Amazon